DUST BABY

I wonder if you've ever had to draw your own family tree at school? It's generally a fun thing to do, especially if you can design it like a real tree, with branches here and there. You can draw a snake slithering round the branch representing your pesky little brother, cute squirrels scampering along the branches symbolizing your favourite cousins and maybe an owl with glasses roosting on the branch for your wise old uncle. But whether you do this funny version, or just use plain lines and your best handwriting, it's generally easy to construct.

I could start with me at the bottom, then have my mother Biddy and my father Harry holding hands above me, and then above them my maternal grandparents, George and Hilda-Ellen, and my paternal grandparents, Harry and Dorothy. After that it gets a bit hazy, but it's a start.

What would happen if you couldn't make that start? How would you feel if you could only put your name on the page? That's what it's like for April, the girl in *Dustbin Baby*. She's not even sure that's the name her mother would have chosen for her. She doesn't have a clue who that mother is. April was abandoned in a dustbin the moment she was born, bundled up and left to die. Thank goodness she cried hard and someone heard and rushed her to hospital. This happened on April 1st, All Fool's Day, when you play jokes on people. April's life hasn't been much of a joke though. She's been sent here, sent there, fostered out, stuck in a children's home, boarded in a special school, until she doesn't know where she is. She doesn't know who she is.

Dustbin Baby takes place all in one day, this momentous fourteenth birthday when April sets out to find herself. I think we all go through a stage of feeling a little odd and alienated from our families at this age. It must be so much harder if you feel you haven't got any family at all.

I felt very close to April when I was writing her story and I struggled hard to make sure she had a happy ending.

Jacqueline Wilson

Jacqueline Wilson

Illustrated by Nick Sharratt

DUSTBIN BABY

CORGI
YEARLING

DUSTBIN BABY
A CORGI BOOK 978 0 552 57119 7

First published in Great Britain by Doubleday,
an imprint of Random House Children's Publishers UK
A Random House Group Company

Doubleday edition published 2001
First Corgi edition published 2002
Reissued 2007
This edition published 2013

3

The Random House Group Limited supports The Forest Stewardship Council®
(FSC®), the leading international forest-certification organisation. Our books
carrying the FSC label are printed on FSC®-certified paper. FSC is the only
forest-certification scheme supported by the leading environmental organisations,
including Greenpeace. Our paper procurement policy can be found at
www.randomhouse.co.uk/environment

MIX
Paper from
responsible sources
FSC® C016897

Set in New Century Schoolbook

Corgi Yearling Books are published by Random House Children's Publishers UK,
61–63 Uxbridge Road, London W5 5SA

www.randomhousechildrens.co.uk
www.totallyrandombooks.co.uk
www.randomhouse.co.uk

Addresses for companies within The Random House Group Limited
can be found at: www.randomhouse.co.uk/offices.htm

THE RANDOM HOUSE GROUP Limited Reg. No. 954009

A CIP catalogue record for this book is available from the British Library.

Printed and bound by CPI Group (UK) Ltd, Croydon, CR0 4YY

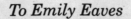

To Emily Eaves

Let's begin with a happy ending.

I sit here in the warm, waiting. I can't eat anything. My mouth is too dry to swallow properly. I try sipping water. The glass clanks against my teeth. My hand is trembling. I put the glass down carefully and then clasp my hands tight. I squeeze until my nails dig in. I need to feel it.

I need to know that this is real.

I think people are staring at me, wondering why I'm all on my own. But not for much longer.

Please come now. Please.

I look out the window, seeing my own pale reflection. And then there's a shadow. Someone stares back at me. And then smiles.

I smile too, though the tears are welling in my eyes. Why do I always have to cry? I mop at my face fiercely with a napkin. When I look back the window is empty.

'April?'

I jump. I look up.

'April, is it really you?

I nod, still crying. I get clumsily to my feet. We look at each other and then our arms go out. We embrace, hugging each other close, even though we are strangers.

'Happy birthday!'

'This is the best birthday ever,' I whisper.

It's nearly over – and yet it's just beginning.

1

I always hate my birthdays. I don't tell anyone that. Cathy and Hannah would think me seriously weird. I try so hard to fit in with them so they'll stay friends with me. Sometimes I try too hard and I find myself copying them.

It's OK if I just yell 'Yay!' like Cathy or dance hunched-up Hannah-style. Ordinary friends catch habits from each other easily enough. But every now and then I overstep this mark in my eagerness. I started reading exactly the same books as Cathy until she spotted what I was doing.

'Can't you choose for yourself, April?' she said. 'Why do you always have to copy me?'

'I'm sorry, Cathy.'

Hannah got irritated too when I started styling my hair exactly like hers, even buying the same little slides and bands and beads.

'This is *my* hairstyle, April,' she said, giving one of my tiny beaded plaits a tug.

'I'm sorry, Hannah.'

They've both started sighing whenever I say sorry.

'It's kind of creepy,' said Cathy. 'You don't have to keep saying sorry to *us*.'

'We're your friends,' said Hannah.

They *are* my friends and I badly want them to stay my friends. They're the first nice normal friends I've ever had. They think I'm nice and normal too, give or take a few slightly strange ways. I'm going to do my best to keep it like that. I'm never going to tell them about me. I'd die if they found out.

I've got so good at pretending I hardly know I'm doing it. I'm like an actress. I've had to play lots and lots of parts. Sometimes I'm not sure if there's any real me left. No, the real me is this me, funny little April Showers, fourteen years old. Today.

I don't know how I'm going to handle it. It's the one day when it's hard to pretend.

Marion asked me last week if I wanted to do anything special. I just shook my head, but so emphatically that my face was hidden by my hair.

Cathy had a sleepover for her fourteenth birthday. We watched spooky videos and one hilarious rude one that gave us the most terrible giggles and put us off having sex for life.

Hannah had a proper party, a disco in a church hall decked out with fairy lights and candles to try to give it atmosphere. There were boys too, but only Hannah's brother and his friends and a few totally sad guys in our year. Still, it was great fun.

I loved Cathy's birthday. I loved Hannah's birthday. It's mine that is the problem.

I just want to get it over and done with.

'Are you sure you don't want a party?' Marion asked.

I can just imagine the sort of party Marion would organize. Charades and Pin-the-Tail-on-the-Donkey and sausages on sticks and fruit punch, like way back when *she* was young.

Maybe that's not fair.

I'm sick of being fair.

I'm sick of *her*.

That's so mean. She's trying so hard.

'Perhaps you and I could go out for a meal somewhere?' she suggested, like it would be a big treat.

'No, honestly, I don't want to make a big deal of my birthday,' I said, yawning, as if the whole subject simply bored me.

Marion's no fool. 'I know birthdays must be difficult for you,' she said softly.

'No, they're OK. *I'm* OK,' I insisted. 'I just don't want you to make a fuss about it.'

She swallowed. Then she looked at me sideways. 'I take it *presents* aren't making too much of a fuss?' she said.

'I like the sound of presents,' I said, snapping out of my sulks.

I looked at her hopefully. I'd hinted enough times. 'What are you giving me?'

'You'll have to wait and see,' said Marion.

'Give me a clue, please!'

'Absolutely not.'

'Go *on*. Is it . . . is it . . . ?' I gestured, holding one hand up to my ear.

'You'll have to wait and see,' said Marion, but she smiled broadly.

I'm sure I've guessed right. Even though she's moaned and groaned about them enough.

Marion wakes me up with a birthday breakfast in bed. I don't actually ever want to bother with breakfast but I sit up and try to look enthusiastic. She's poured far too much milk on my cornflakes but she's added strawberries too, and she's put a little bunch of baby irises in a champagne flute to match the willow pattern china. There's a present on the tray, a neat rectangle, *just* the right size.

'Oh Marion!' I say, leaning forward, almost ready to hug her.

Milk splashes all over the sheets as the tray tilts. 'Careful, careful!' Marion goes, snatching the present to safety.

'Hey, it's mine!' I say, taking it from her. It feels a little light. Maybe it's one of those really neat tiny ones. I undo the ribbon and rip off the paper. Marion automatically smoothes the paper and winds the ribbon neatly round and round her fingers. I take the lid off the cardboard box – and there's another smaller box. I take the lid off this box and find another even smaller box. Too small, surely.

I remember someone playing a trick on one of the kids in Sunnybank. They opened up box after box after box. There was nothing at all in the matchbox at the end and everyone laughed. I did, too, though I wanted to cry.

'Go on, open the next box,' says Marion.

'Is it a joke?' I asked. Surely she wouldn't play games with me like that?

'I didn't want you to guess what it was too easily. But I think you know. Open it, April.'

So I open it. It's the last box. There's a present inside. But it's the *wrong* present.

'It's earrings!'

'Do you like them? They're blue moon-stones. I thought they'd bring out the blue of your eyes.'

I barely hear her. I feel *so* disappointed. I was *sure* she was giving me a mobile. She smiled when I gestured . . . Then I realize. She thought I was pointing at my newly-pierced ears.

The fancy earrings are a peace-offering. She made such a fuss when Cathy and Hannah egged me on one Saturday and I got my ears pierced in Claire's Accessories. You'd have thought I'd had my tongue pierced the way she was carrying on.

'What's the matter?' she asks. 'Don't you like the moonstones?'

'Yes. They're lovely. It's just . . .' I can't keep it in any more. 'I thought I was getting a mobile phone.'

Marion stares at me. 'Oh April! You know what I think about mobiles.'

I know all right. She's gone on and on and on about all these stupid brain tumour scares and the whole big bore social nuisance factor. As if I care! I just want my own mobile like every other girl my age. Cathy got a mobile for her fourteenth birthday. Hannah got a mobile for her fourteenth birthday. Every girl everywhere gets a mobile for her fourteenth birthday, if not before. All the Year Nine girls have got mobiles. And most of Year Eight.

I feel like I'm the only one anywhere without any means of communication. I can't natter or send funny text messages or take calls from my friends. I can't join in. I'm the odd one out.

I always am.

'I wanted a mobile!' I wail like a baby.

'Oh for God's sake, April,' says Marion. 'You know perfectly well what I think about mobiles. I *hate* them.'

'I don't!'

'They're an absolutely outrageous invention – those ridiculous little tunes tinkling everywhere, and idiots announcing "Hello, I'm on the train" as if anyone cares!'

'*I* care. I want to keep in touch with my friends.'

'Don't be silly. You see them every day.'

'Cathy is always sending text messages to

Hannah and she sends them back and they're always laughing away together and *I'm* always left out – because I haven't got a mobile.'

'Well, that's tough, April. You'll just have to learn to live with it. I've told you and told you—'

'Oh yeah, you've told me all right.'

'Please don't talk in that silly sulky tone, it's incredibly irritating.'

'I can't help it if you think I'm irritating. I don't see that it's so terrible to want a mobile phone when it's what every single teenager in the entire *world* owns without question.'

'Don't be so ridiculous.'

'*Why* is it so ridiculous? I just want to be like my friends. Cathy's got a mobile. Hannah's got a mobile. Why can't *I* have a mobile?'

'I've just *told* you why.'

'Yes, well, I'm sick of you telling me this and telling me that. Who are you to tell me all this stuff? It's not like you're my *mother*.'

'Look, I try—'

'But I don't *want* you to!'

My mouth says it all of its own accord. There's suddenly a silence in the room.

I didn't mean it.

Yes I did.

Marion sits down heavily on the end of my bed. I look at my breakfast tray. I look at my blue moonstone earrings.

I could say I'm sorry. I could say sweet things to her. I could eat up my cornflakes. I could screw my new earrings into my ears and give Marion a big kiss and tell her I just love the blue moonstones.

Only I wish they were a mobile phone. I don't see why that's so wicked. I mean honestly, a *mobile*! Doesn't she want me to keep in touch with everyone?

Maybe she wants me all to herself. Well, I don't want *her*.

I get up, I leave my breakfast tray, I go into the bathroom, locking the door on Marion. I want to shut her out of my life. I don't want to wear her silly little moonstone earrings. I was into fancy earrings *months* ago, when I kept nagging to have my ears pierced. Can't she keep a track of things? I am so sick of her and the way she never manages to get things right.

I get washed. I get dressed. Marion's gone downstairs. I wish I could sidle out of the house without having to face her. I don't see why she always has to make me feel so guilty. It's not my fault. I didn't ask her to take care of me. I'm not going to wear the earrings. I don't want those twinkly little-girly earrings clogging up my earlobes. I'm sick of thinking about her and her feelings.

She's bending down by the front door, picking up the post. My heart leaps. There are three birthday cards – but not the one I'm looking for. Though it's silly, *she* doesn't know my address. Maybe she doesn't even know my name. How could she ever get in touch?

Marion is watching me. Her face is all creased up with sympathy. This makes me feel even worse. 'April, I know it's hard for you. I do understand.'

'No, you *don't*!'

She presses her lips together until they nearly disappear. Then she breathes heavily through her nose like a horse.

'I know this is a difficult day for you but there's no need to shout at me. You're acting like a sulky little brat. You haven't even thanked me properly for the earrings.'

'Thank you!'

It comes out even more rudely than I intended. I feel tears of shame prickling my eyes. I don't want to hurt her.

Yes I do.

'I'm sick of having to say please and thank you all the time and acting all prissy and posh. I don't want to be like you. I just want to be *me*,' I say, and I barge past her, out the front door, off to school. I don't even say goodbye.

I don't want to think about Marion any more because it makes me feel so bad. I'll wall her up right at the back of my mind. There are a lot of other people squashed in there in the dark.

I think about me. I don't know how to be me when I'm by myself. I don't know who I am. There's only one person who can tell me and she's got no way of getting in touch.

I think about it.

I go into the paper shop on the corner. Raj grins at me. 'Hi, April.'

I walk past the chocolate, the crisps, the fizzy drinks. I look at the newspapers in neat black-and-white rows. *The Times*. That's the one with the Personal column. We divided it up between us in Media Studies and had to analyse each section.

I can't really search through the whole paper looking for it. Raj has pained little messages pinned up on his shelves. 'I am not a lending library. No looking without purchasing'.

So I'll purchase. Raj pulls a funny face. 'Getting all serious and intellectual, April?' he says.

'That's right,' I say.

'It's a joke, right? For April Fool?'

'No, I really want to buy it.'

'You girls,' says Raj, as if I'm playing an elaborate trick on him.

He doesn't know, but I don't ever play April Fool jokes. No wastepaper baskets balanced on top of doors, no drawing pins on chairs, no 'Watch out, what's that behind you?' On my birthday I always feel there's really something about to fall on me, that someone's creeping up on me. I long for it to happen.

I give Raj the money for the paper. He peers at the coins suspiciously, checking whether they're chocolate. I've fooled him all right. My trick is that there's no trick.

There's no message either. I lean against the wall outside the shop and struggle with the flapping pages. April is a windy month. I wish I'd been born at another time of the year. What a birthday – April Fool's Day. Talk about a sick joke.

Some of the messages in the Personal column could be cryptic jokes. They make no sense to me. But there's nothing from her. No 'Happy Birthday – I always think of you on April 1st'. Does she? I always think of her. I don't know what she's really like of course. But I can imagine.

I'm good at imagining.

Whenever we have History and we have to imagine what it would feel like to be a Roman centurion or a Tudor queen or a London child in the Blitz I can always pretend I'm there and I can write it all down and Mrs Hunter gives me excellent marks. Even though I'm imagining so hard I forget about paragraphs and punctuation and my spelling goes all to pot.

But it's OK at this school. Everything's fine. I've caught up. It's not like some of the other schools where they thought I was really thick or mad or they knew all about me and the teachers whispered and raised their eyebrows and the kids teased me and called me names. Oh God, I sound as if I should be playing my violin, *sooooo* sorry for poor little me.

I'm not poor, though I *am* little. No one knows about me at this school. I'm just April and I'm in Year Nine and people only know me because I'm the girl with the long fair hair who goes round with Cathy and Hannah. No-one thinks I'm odd, although I get teased a bit for being a crybaby. I howled in class the other day when we were told about destitute child refugees, without their parents. I was still blubbering at breaktime. Cathy had her arm round me and Hannah was mopping my eyes with a wad of tissues when a teacher walking past got all fussed and asked if I was unwell. Hannah said, 'It's just April, she's always crying,' and Cathy said, 'We call her April Showers.'

That's my nickname now. It's better than April Fool.

It's much, much better than Dustbin Baby.

That's the real me. I was in the newspapers. I suppose it's a special claim to fame. Not many people make the front page the day they're born. But not many people get chucked out like rubbish. One look and it's, 'No way, don't want this baby, let's chuck her in the dustbin.'

Funny kind of cradle. A pizza box for a pillow, newspaper as a coverlet, scrunched-up tissues serving as a mattress.

What kind of mother could dump her own baby in a dustbin?

No, I'm not being fair. I don't think it was just that she couldn't stand the sight of me. She was probably scared silly. Maybe no one else knew about the baby and she didn't dare tell anyone?

Imagine.

Why doesn't she want me? She's on her own. She can't look after me. She's very young. That's why she can't keep me.

So the pains start and she doesn't know what to do. Maybe she's still at school. She clutches her tummy and gasps and the girl next to her asks if she's all right. She can't say, 'Oh, don't worry, I'm just having a baby and it's absolute agony.' So maybe she just shakes her head and says she's got a bad stomach ache. Maybe she makes out it's that time of the month. Maybe that's what she really thinks! Maybe she doesn't even know she's having a baby?

No, she does know, deep down, but it's so scary she's not let herself think about it. She hasn't made any plans at all because she can't face up to it. Even now, when she can feel me struggling to get out of her, she doesn't quite believe that I exist.

It doesn't seem real at all, sitting in her lesson at school. I wonder what she likes best? Is it History, like me? Is she clever? Does she have a lot of friends? Maybe not. Not a friend close enough to tell. Maybe she's quite a big girl and no one's really looked at her closely and noticed that she's put on a lot of weight. She's worn large, loose jumpers and skived off PE and somehow got away with it.

What about at home though? What about her mum?

Maybe her mum doesn't bother about her much. Maybe she's scared of her dad. That's why she hasn't told. She isn't close to anyone at home.

That's how it happened. She isn't the silly sort of girl who sleeps around. She's quiet and shy. She's not really popular with boys but a while ago – OK, nine months ago – she was at a party, feeling a bit out of it, all set to make some excuse about having to go home early, but then this boy she's never seen before, someone's cousin, comes and sits down beside her, talking to her as if he really wants to get to know her.

They can scarcely hear each other because the music is so loud so they go in the kitchen and have a few drinks together. She's not used to drinking, only had a few sips of wine and a can or two of lager before, she hasn't liked the taste, but now she's drinking something sweet, with fruit salad floating on top, and it slips down as easily as anything and makes her feel good. The boy makes her feel good too. He's holding her hand now, his head close to hers, and they have another drink, and another. There are too many people in the kitchen so they take their next drinks out into the garden.

It was so hot in the kitchen she felt her face glowing as pink as her drink but it's cold outdoors and she starts shivering. He puts his arm round her to warm her up.

'Do you believe in love at first sight?' he says, and then he kisses her. She can't believe this is happening to her at last. It's too perfect, too beautiful, but then it starts to get too hasty, too worrying. What is he doing? No, she doesn't want to, not that, please don't. Please, he says, you know you want to really. I love you, he says. It's the first time anyone's ever said 'I love you,' and so she lets him love her and then it's all over and he walks away and leaves her lying there in the garden all by herself.

She can't find him when she stops crying and tidies herself and goes back into the house. She searches upstairs and downstairs. She asks people if they've seen him. He's called . . .

I don't know. Maybe *she* doesn't even know. He's disappeared anyway. So she goes home and cries some more in bed and when she wakes up the next morning it's as if it's all been a dream. She isn't sure it really did happen.

She doesn't forget him. She thinks about him all day and half the night but he stops being a real person to her. It's as if he's a rock star, someone to daydream about.

She doesn't think about *babies*. You don't get pregnant if you have a vivid dream or fantasize about a boy in a band. But the weeks go by. Then the months. She knows perfectly well that there are all sorts of changes going on in her body but she doesn't want to think about them. Every time anything too scary crosses her mind she sings her favourite songs over and over to blot out the worries. Of course it's not real. It can't happen to her.

But it *is* happening. It's April 1st and she can't keep still on her chair. She's scared she's going to have an awful accident in public, so she staggers to her feet and tells her teacher that she feels bad. She looks so white and sweaty that the teacher thinks she'd better go home.

She doesn't go home. Her mum will be sprawled on the sofa watching television. She doesn't know where she can go. The pain's getting worse. It's not just in her stomach. It's growing, taking her over altogether, so that on the bus into town she can't sit still, she can't stop herself groaning. She has to get up before her usual stop and is sick in the gutter the second she steps off the bus.

She wonders if this can really be the reason for the pain, a simple stomach bug making her sick, but the pain is still there, the bug is getting bigger and bigger, battling inside her until she can hardly stand. People are staring at her so she drags herself away, making for the Ladies' room in the shopping centre. She locks herself in the cubicle and lets herself groan the way she wants, but she can hear muttering outside and after a minute or two there's a knock on the door.

'Are you all right in there?'

She says nothing, hoping that they might just go away, but they keep on knocking. She hears keys jangling. They'll come barging right in. 'I've got this tummy bug,' she gasps.

'Shall I call for the store nurse?'

'No! No, I'm OK now. I'm coming out.'

She takes a deep breath, praying for the pain to stop for a minute, and gets herself out the door, past their gawping faces, shuffling right out the Ladies', looking for somewhere, anywhere, she can be alone.

She staggers through the shopping centre, out the back, round behind the cinema. She's making for another Ladies' toilet, one where there won't be an attendant. It's down an alleyway by a restaurant called The Pizza Place. She has to get there though she can barely walk now. She just wants to push this bug out of her.

The Ladies' is shut up, locked and barred. She can't go anywhere else. It's too late. She can't wait, it's coming, she can feel it.

She crouches behind the dustbins belonging to The Pizza Place, she pulls off her underclothes, pushing, pushing, pushing – and then suddenly I am born in a hot slippery rush.

I am there in her cupped hands, I'm not like the little pink powdery babies in adverts. I am newborn, purple as a plum, slimy and strange. I'm still not real. I'm an alien attached to her body.

Do I cry?

Maybe she cries, sobbing with shock as she ransacks her schoolbag and finds a penknife, rubber bands, and then clamps the scary cord and detaches us.

Detaches us for ever.

She looks at me.

I look back.

If only I could remember what she looks like now.

I look and look and look in this new bright blurry world.

Her hands hold me.

She picks me up properly.

She doesn't cuddle me close. She opens a

dustbin with one hand and drops me in with the other.

Then the lid goes down.

It is dark.

I have lost her for ever.

2

So there I am. In the dustbin in the dark.

What do I do?

Cry, of course. I'm April Showers.

I've got a mouth like a Polo mint and lungs the size of teaspoons but I do my best. I wail and shriek and yell, my face screwed up, my knees against my chest, my fists flailing.

But the lid is on top. My little bleats are muffled. Who's listening anyway? She's gone.

No one comes down this alley any more now the Ladies' toilets are closed.

I don't give up. I cry and cry and cry until I'm as red as a raspberry, the veins standing out on my forehead, my wisps of hair damp with effort. I am damp all over because I have no nappy. I have no clothes at all and if I stop crying I will become dangerously cold.

I cry though she's not coming back. I cry though it hurts my throat. I cry though my eyes are shut and I am getting so tired that all I want to do is give up and sleep. But I'm not going to give up. I cry . . .

And then someone tugs at the lid.

'Kitty? Are you trapped inside? Hang on, I'll get you out.'

Sudden light. Pink blur. A face. Not hers. A man. No, it's a boy. Frankie. He works the evening shift at The Pizza Place to help out while he's at college, though of course I don't know this yet. He's just Someone and I wail desperately for help.

'A baby!' He backs away warily as if I'm dangerous, his mouth hanging open. He drops the rubbish he's carried from the kitchen.

He shakes his head as if he can't believe in me, then touches me with one fingertip, checking I'm real . . .

'You poor little thing!' His hands go right round me, clumsy but very gentle. He lifts me up and looks at me.

She looked at me too. I wait for him to drop me back in the dustbin. But he tenderly tucks me down inside his shirt, in the warm, even though I am damp and dirty.

'There now,' he says, cradling me, then he hurries back up the alley into the kitchens, looking as if he's suddenly grown a beer belly.

'What you got there, Frankie?' one of the women asks. Alice. She's old enough to be Frankie's mum but they're pals.

'A baby,' he says, really quietly so as not to startle me, though there's a clatter and clash from all corners of the kitchen.

'Oh sure,' she says. 'What is it? Did someone chuck a doll in the dustbins?'

'Look,' says Frankie, leaning forward so she can see into his shirt.

I murmur as he shifts, trying to clutch his skin with my tiny fists.

'Oh my lord!' Alice shrieks, so loudly that everyone comes running.

There's a babble all around me and fingers poke.

'Don't! You're frightening her. I think she's hungry,' says Frankie. 'Look at her little mouth. It's like she's looking for something.'

'Something you haven't got, Frankie!'

'What about some milk?' says Frankie. 'We could heat her up some milk.'

'She's too little. Newborn. We'd better call an ambulance,' says Alice. 'And the police.'

'Police?'

'Well, someone's dumped her, haven't they? Here, Frankie, let me take her.'

'No. I want to hold her. I found her. She likes me, look.'

I do like Frankie. If I can't have a mum perhaps he'll do for a dad. I start shrieking when the ambulance men arrive and try to take me out of his shirt. I want his warmth, his skin, his care.

'See, she *does* like me,' Frankie says proudly.

He tucks me back inside his shirt and

comes in the ambulance with me. He stays at the hospital while the paediatrician checks me all over and waits while a nurse baths me and then wraps me up.

'Here, Frankie, you can give the baby her first feed,' she says.

She sits him down and puts me back in his arms. I liked it better inside his shirt against his skin but this way still feels good though I can't snuggle properly in my new stiff sleeping suit. Frankie touches my mouth with the rubber teat of the feeding bottle. I fasten on it at once. I don't need to be shown how to suck. I know straight away. Once I start I can't stop. Everything blurs. I forget my mother. I forget the hospital and the doctor and nurses. I even forget Frankie. It's just the bottle and me. I want to suck for ever. And then I sleep ... And when I wake up Frankie isn't there.

I cry. He doesn't come back.

Nurses come. Nurses go.

Maybe, I think, this is the way it is. No one ever stays. But the magic bottle appears regularly so I concentrate on that.

Then suddenly familiar hands scoop me

out of my cot and I'm back down a shirt, my cheek against skin, Frankie's skin. He's come back for me.

Of course he hasn't *really*. This is for the newspapers. I think I even make it onto television too, though no one videoed it. Well. She might have. My mother.

Did she keep the photos when they were published the next day in the newspapers? Did she snip out the features?

DUSTBIN BABY

College student Frankie Smith, 17, found a surprise waiting for him when he did his evening shift at The Pizza Place in the High Street yesterday. He heard a high-pitched wailing coming from the refuse bins at the back of the popular restaurant.

'I thought it was a cat,' said Frankie. 'I got the shock of my life when I took the dustbin lid off and saw the baby.' Frankie has two young brothers of his own and has done his fair share of babysitting – so he had no qualms about looking after the baby, keeping it warm by tucking the tiny infant inside his shirt.

Frankie accompanied her to St Mary's Hospital, where doctors examined the baby and said she is in perfect health in spite of her ordeal in the dustbin. They believe she was only minutes old when she was abandoned. Her mother will be in need of medical attention. She is urged to contact St Mary's Hospital as soon as possible, where she can be reunited with her daughter.

The baby was naked, not even wearing a nappy, and so far there are no clues to her identity. She is white, with fair hair, and weighs a healthy 6 lbs. Nurses at the hospital say she is adorable. She's been named April because she was found on April 1st.

'I certainly thought someone was playing a joke on me,' beamed Frankie, cuddling little baby April in his arms. 'If her mother doesn't want her I wish I could look after her!'

I wish it too, Frankie.

I wish you were still seventeen. I wonder how we'd get on? I'm still little, the smallest girl in my class, the smallest in every class I've ever been in, and that takes some serious counting. I'm skinny too, though Marion's been trying desperately hard to fatten me up. She's particularly keen on milk: on my corn-flakes, mushed up with muesli, whipped into Angel Delight, baked into rice pudding, stirred into cocoa, shaken with strawberry ice-cream. She's inventive, all right, and it seems so mean to screw my face up and shudder, but I hate milk now, even though I used to suck the stopper off my baby bottles. So I'm seriously small, Frankie, but you could hardly tuck me inside your shirt now.

I wonder what it would feel like? I wonder if you've got a hairy chest now and a real beer belly? You're thirty-one. You've probably got babies of your own.

You look lovely in the photo in the paper. I've looked at it so many times it's a wonder there's any image left. I've peered at it so closely that your face and mine blur into thousands of little dots on the yellowing page. You can only see my head. The rest of me is inside your shirt.

My eyes are open and I'm looking straight

at you. OK, I'm a little squinty from all the flashbulbs but I'm looking up and you're looking down at me. You've got this lovely smile as if I'm really special. Maybe the photographers told you to look that way so it would make a great picture. Maybe you really felt it. Though if that was the case why didn't you keep in touch? Maybe they wouldn't let you, especially after I was adopted. Maybe you really tried to see me. Maybe you weren't joking when you said you wished you could look after me.

They don't let seventeen-year-old boys look after abandoned baby girls. It's weird. If my mother had gone rushing to the hospital begging to be reunited with me they'd probably have let her look after me. Even though she threw me in the dustbin and shut the lid on me. But that's because we're related. Blood is thicker than water. She's the only blood relative that I know about and yet of course I know nothing at all about her.

I can't stop thinking about her. Well, not *all* the time. I'm happy. I've got a new life. Lots of people like me. I've got a home. I love my new school and my best friends Cathy and Hannah . . .

I wonder what they're giving me for my birthday? Cathy will probably give me a book. Not a kid's one. She'll pick one of those girly books with bright covers and lots of detailed description of love sessions inside. She might well have read it first, but I shan't mind a bit. We'll all go into a huddle in the playground and read little snippets out loud and get the giggles.

Hannah will probably give me make-up. No, nail varnish, a really funky colour, and we'll give each other a manicure at lunchtime and paint our nails.

Lunch will be especially good too. We all take packed lunches and mine is always particularly boring. (Marion goes in for wedges of wholemeal bread and cheese and carrots and yogurt and bananas and sultanas, like I'm a very special kind of monkey.) However, Cathy and Hannah and I have this tradition that whenever it's our birthday we nip out to the bakery for big cream doughnuts.

My mouth waters now thinking about the doughnuts as I walk to school. I never ate my birthday breakfast. I want to have my birthday doughnut, I want to see Cathy and Hannah, I want my birthday to be fun like anyone else's birthday. But I'm not anyone else. I'm me.

I walk on, past the school, hurrying now in case anyone spots me. I start running. I can't go to school today. I can't go home. I have to go *back*.

3

'You can't look back. You have to look forwards.' That's what Cathy said, very firmly.
But she wasn't talking about me, of course,
she was saying it to Hannah. It was just
about this boy Hannah once went out with. I
say 'just'. It was Grant Lacey. If you went to
our school you'd be seriously impressed. Even
his name sounds special, like he's a rock star
or a famous footballer. The way the girls go on

about him you'd really think he is. He might even get to be famous one day. He plays in the school orchestra, classical stuff and a bit of jazz for concerts, but we've all heard him riffing on his guitar at break. He's really great, fast and furious, though he can be soulful when he wants to, singing along with his eyes looking straight at you as if he's in love with you. He's great at football too. Maybe not ultra-talented like the really sporty jocks, but they're just pathetic, terrible show-offs and much too muscly. Grant is in the school football team, partly because he's so popular – and partly because he's got great legs, lean and shapely and strong and every girl in our school wants to ogle them.

Well, that's what the girls say. I say so too and act as if I'm crazy about Grant like Hannah and Cathy and everyone else but privately I think he's a stupid show-off. I don't even think he looks that great. He's handsome. *Too* handsome. You know when you turn the colour tone too high on the television and all the reds glow lobster and the green is like the grass in Teletubby land? Someone's turned the tone up inside Grant, so his face is too chiselled and clean cut, his hair too blond, his eyes too blue, his teeth too white in his perfect smile. That smile! I bet he practises it every night in his bathroom mirror. One corner of his lips quirks upwards, the other has just the hint of a droop so that he doesn't look too eager. The smile of the super-cool. He smiled at Hannah and she came running.

We were all surprised. Cathy and I are used to boys making a play for Hannah, of course. They look straight *past* Cathy and me. Cathy is big and bouncy and pounces on people in a friendly fashion like Tigger. I'm more like Piglet, little and pink, and I sometimes wear my hair in a pigtail too. Hannah is more of a Barbie doll than a cuddly toy. She's blonde like Barbie, and she's got that sort of figure too. Boys are always hanging round Hannah. Boys in our year at school, not Year Eleven like Grant. But Hannah sings in the choir and they get to practise with the orchestra sometimes after school, and a few weeks ago Grant casually suggested to Hannah that she might like to go to McDonald's afterwards on their way home.

Hannah is a vegetarian and disapproves of McDonald's — but she'd have eaten a whole cow raw if Grant had suggested it. So off they went to McDonald's and Hannah nibbled a few chips in total seventh heaven — *seventy*-seventh heaven, stars shining overhead and herds of little cows jumping over a galaxy of moons. Grant walked home with Hannah, going right out of his way to do so. Hannah said her heart was thumping like crazy wondering whether he was going to kiss her when he said goodbye. She wanted him to kiss her *sooooo* badly and yet she was terrified too, wishing she could brush her teeth and put lipgloss on first.

She kept up a frantic gabble all the way down her road right up to her front door. Grant gave her his much-practised devastating smile, bent his head — and kissed her.

Hannah held her breath. She told us it felt wonderful, but she was so worked up she was scared she might laugh or cry, and she was starting to feel dizzy not breathing. Grant looked deep into her eyes and she was so overcome she let it all go and *snorted* right in his face. He leapt backwards in alarm and he looked so comical she carried on giggling helplessly, spluttering and gasping, going into peal after peal of laughter.

'I'm so sorry,' she gasped, clutching her sides.

Grant gave her one cool look of contempt and walked off. She tried calling after him but he didn't even look back.

She knew she'd blown it and burst into tears. She tried apologizing properly the next day at school but Grant just raised an eyebrow.

'I didn't realize you're just a silly little kid,' he said and he sauntered off.

He ignored her completely after that. Poor Hannah was heartbroken. She wrote to him but he didn't reply. She plucked up all her courage and phoned him, leaving sad little messages on his answerphone, but he never called her back. She invited him to her fourteenth birthday party but he didn't turn up.

'If only I hadn't been so *stupid*,' Hannah wailed. 'How could I have acted like such an idiot? Snorting right in his face! And all this stuff came out my *nose*. I just about died when I saw myself in the mirror. He must have thought he was with a total loony, laughing like a jackass with green slime dripping out my nostrils!'

I gave poor Hannah a hug and Cathy launched into her speech about not looking back, looking forward . . .

But it was Hannah's mum who was really comforting. She was so sweet at Hannah's disco, boogying away just like us most of the evening, but when nearly everyone had gone home and Hannah had started crying because she'd so hoped Grant would turn up after all, Hannah's mum put her arms round her and stroked her hair out of her eyes and kissed her on the nose and told her she was worth ten of Grant Lacey and she'd pull *vastly* superior boys in the future.

I started crying too and everyone thought it was me doing my usual April Showers act, sad for poor Hannah. Well, I was sad for her – but I was also so jealous it's a wonder I didn't gleam emerald green all over. I wasn't jealous of Hannah because of Grant Lacey. I was jealous of Hannah because she had a lovely mum.

I'm even jealous of Cathy and *her* mum, though she's a terrible worryguts who's on the phone flapping if Cathy is five minutes late home from school and she calls her seriously embarrassing baby nicknames like Cuddlepie and Chubbychops. Cathy squirms when she does it in front of us. I shake my head sympathetically but I have to blink hard to stop tears spilling down my cheeks.

I want a mum to cuddle and kiss me. I want a mum to worry about me. I want a mum to baby me.

I don't say a word about it to Cathy and Hannah of course. They think I've *got* a mum. They've only met Marion a couple of times. Maybe they were surprised that she's much older than their mums but they didn't say anything. They seemed to think it cool that I call her by her first name.

'Did you call Marion "Mum" when you were little?' Cathy asked.

I fudged things by saying I'd always called her Marion.

I can't start calling Marion 'Mum' now.

I've called lots of women 'Mum'. I don't even remember what the first one looked like. Patricia Williams. That's the name in my file. It's a huge great box file packed with all kinds of clippings and letters and reports. It's got my name on it but I wasn't even allowed to have one quick peep inside – not until I went to live with Marion. She insisted. She said she didn't care what the rules were, it was my basic moral right to learn about my past. Marion's great at getting her own way, even with senior social workers. She doesn't shout. She doesn't even argue. She just states things quietly but firmly. So they gave in and presented me with my brimming box file. *Dustbin Baby, This Is Your Life.*

I knew lots of it already, of course. I'd made a scrapbook of my life when I was little. They don't like you using the word 'scrapbook' because they don't want you to feel you're like little throwaway scrappy bits of paper. Though that's the way I *do* feel. You know those linked dolls you can make if you fold a piece of paper and cut out a girl shape? They all look identical but you can colour them all in differently and put glasses on one and bright lipstick on another and choose varying patterns for their dresses. I'm like all those paper dolls. I've stayed the same shape girl all my life but each time I've gone to a new home someone's coloured me in differently.

Patricia Williams was my first mum, though she wasn't permanent. She took in foster kids. She'd been doing it for years, babies a speciality, so they took me out of hospital when I was a few days old and she looked after me until I was nearly one.

I wonder if she remembers me? If only I could remember her! I have these dreams where someone's lifting me up and holding me close and kissing me. Cathy's got a dream journal and writes all her dreams down. We were all discussing our dreams one day, cosily squashed up together in a corner of the playground, and just this once I forgot to be cautious and started telling them about my recurring dream. Luckily they started hooting with laughter long before I was finished, totally misinterpreting everything, thinking

I was dreaming about a romantic encounter with some boy. I let them carry on thinking that because it was less embarrassing than the truth. Normal people don't dream about being babies. I don't know who the dream arms belonged to. Not my mother. She didn't hold me close and kiss me. She probably seized me by the ankles and shoved me straight in the dustbin.

So have I been dreaming about this first foster mother, Mrs Williams? I've got an idea of her in my head, big and soft and smelling of toast and fresh ironing. I wish she'd pick me up in her arms now. OK, it's crazy. But I want her so.

I'm going to try to see her. I've got her address from the file. She's probably moved away ages ago but I still want to see the house. It might feel familiar. And if she is still there I might recognize her.

I know I shouldn't just take off on my own.

I should discuss it properly with Marion. But I don't want to tell her anything. She'd want to take me herself. I don't want to go with her. I want to do it by myself.

It's weird. I haven't really gone anywhere by myself before. Well, I nip down to the corner shops to get the paper for Marion, and I've been trusted to buy a sliced wholemeal loaf and a jar of Gold Blend, and I sometimes choose a video but that's as far as I go, apart from school.

I mooch around the shops with Cathy and Hannah some Saturdays and we go to films together and we went to the under-eighteens' night at the Glitzy once (total disaster – some girls thought Hannah's way of dancing pretty wacky and laughed at her, some other girls thought Cathy was eyeing up one of their boyfriends and threatened her, and one of the bouncers inside refused to believe I was fourteen – well, I was *nearly* – and asked us all to go). Even then we didn't go home by ourselves; Cathy's dad came and collected us and got dead worried when he discovered all *three* of us in tears.

I'm not really used to sorting out trains and stuff. Still, Mrs Williams lives in Weston and that's only a few stops on the train. No problem.

4

Pat Williams

No problem indeed! Weston is *huge* and I don't have a map. I ask about twenty different people if they know the road. I get sent right out of the town, then I'm told that's all wrong and get sent back again. I'm directed down leafy streets near the river with big posh houses and I start to think I started my life in suburban splendour, but I end up in an Avenue rather than a Road and realize this isn't it either. Eventually I trudge all the way back to the railway station and take a taxi. I've got a few pounds in coins and a five-pound note in my school bag. I'm only in the taxi a few minutes but the fare comes to £2.80. I offer the driver three pounds, thinking that will be fine, but he says something dead sarcastic about the generosity of my tip. I end up apologizing and give him the five-pound note instead. He asks if I want any change. I do, but I don't dare say yes, so he just drives off, leaving me feeling flushed and foolish.

A girl with bright orange spiky hair is sitting on the garden wall watching me. She's wearing a very short skirt and a tight T-shirt that shows her tummy. She's got a tiny rainbow arcing over her navel. I *think* it's felt tip but it could just be a real tattoo, though maybe she's not much older than me.

She's got a baby in her arms, a squirming damp bundle, dribbling and whining. He's large and lumpy but she flips him over expertly so he lies across her bony knees, chuckling as she pretends to smack his bottom.

'You must have more money than sense,' she says. 'Feel free to lob a few pounds my way.' But she smiles as she says it.

I smile back. I can't help staring at the baby, wondering.

'He's my third,' she says. 'My other two are at nursery school.' Then she cracks up laughing when she sees my face.

'Joke!'

'Oh!'

'It's April Fool's Day, right?'

'Yeah, right,' I say. 'It's my birthday, actually.'

'Oh well, happy birthday! What's your name?'

'Guess.'

'Oh-oh! April?'

'Yep. What's yours?'

'Tanya.'

The baby gurgles on her lap.

'Yeah, mate, OK. He's saying his name's Ricky.'

The baby squeals excitedly when she says his name and then drools all down Tanya's leg.

'Yuck!' says Tanya, taking off one of his woolly booties and using it as a mop. Then she squints up at me with her small green eyes.

'Are you bunking off school?'

'No.'

'Oh, come on. You're in your school uniform, idiot.'

'OK. Are you bunking off too?'

'I haven't *got* a school at the moment. They're still sorting me out. Don't let's get started on me. There are huge casebooks and files and folders on *me*.' She says it proudly, chin in the air. 'So. What are you here for? Come to see Pat?'

'I don't know,' I mumble. 'Pat? Is she . . . Patricia Williams?'

'That's her. Auntie Pat to all the little kids. Oh, I get it. Were you once one of them?' She laughs. 'Quick on the uptake, that's me. Still, you don't look like one of Pat's kids. Or sound like it either.'

I swallow. I've started talking carefully again since I've been living with Marion. 'I'm just talking posh to impress you, right?' I say, in my old Children's Home voice.

She laughs. 'Yeah, you're quick on the uptake too, April. So, do you want to come in and meet Pat?'

'Maybe it's not such a good idea,' I say, scared all of a sudden.

'She's OK,' says Tanya. 'Come on.'

She stands up, slinging the baby on one hip. She tugs my arm with her free hand. I let her pull me to the front door.

It's on the latch. Tanya kicks it open with her high-heeled sandal. The hall is shabby, with scribbles on the wallpaper and bits of Lego and little cars all over the carpet. The house smells of cooking and nappies and washing powder. I breathe in, wondering if this smell is familiar.

'Pat? We've got a visitor,' Tanya calls, pulling me along the hall into the kitchen.

This woman is standing by the stove, while two little boys bang saucepans at her feet. She's just how I imagined her; soft, cosy, pink cheeks, no make-up, old jumper, baggy denim skirt, scuffed shoes. But there's no prickling at the back of my neck, no tingle at all. I don't recognize her. She doesn't recognize me either, though she smiles cheerfully.

'Hello, dear,' she says. 'Who are you then?'

'I'm April,' I say. I wait.

'April,' she says brightly. 'That's a lovely name. And appropriate for today.'

'That's why I'm called it. Don't you remember? I'm April the Dustbin Baby.' I hate saying it. It sounds so stupid. Sad. Totally pathetic. I feel like I've been shoved right back in the dustbin with the rubbish rotting around me.

'What are you on about, April? What dustbin?' Tanya asks.

'That's where they found me. The day I was born,' I mumble.

'Oh. Right. Cosy,' says Tanya, raising her eyebrows.

'Yes, of course. I remember you now,' says Pat, shaking her head and smiling. 'You were small but very noisy. You cried a lot at night. I walked you up and down, up and down, but you just went on crying. Three-month colic – though it lasted much longer.'

'Maybe she was missing her mum,' says Tanya. 'Did she *really* dump you in a dustbin, April?'

I nod, hoping I'm not going to cry now.

'Dead maternal, your mum,' says Tanya. 'Didn't she like the look of you then?'

'Now then, Tanya, I'd have thought you of all people would know better. You don't talk about other people's families like that. Who are we to pass judgement?' says Pat. 'Some women get very sick when they have babies. Sick in the head. They can't cope. They leave their babies in all sorts of strange places. Telephone boxes. I even had one poor little lamb left in a lavatory.'

'I hope you gave it a good wash before taking it home,' says Tanya. 'Hear that, Ricky? You'd better stop dribbling on me, matie, or it's down to the bottom of the bog for you.'

'Tanya!' says Pat, clucking. 'You stir my mince for me while I fix you both a drink.'

'Bacardi and Coke for me, Pat. What do you fancy, April?' says Tanya.

'Sure. Bacardi and Coke. Only funny thing, we're clean out of Bacardi,' says Pat. 'Do you want a Coke too, April?'

'Yes, please.'

'Where do you live now, dear? Do they

know you're here?' She's trying to sound casual but she's obviously checking up on me. 'You've not done a bunk, have you?'

'Oh, no. I – I had a dental appointment near here and so I thought I'd just come and see where I used to live.'

'Isn't that nice! Well, like I said, I definitely remember you, April.'

She doesn't. She really doesn't. I've just been one of dozens of babies through the years and we've all merged into one little wailing waif. 'Who are you living with now then?' Tanya asks. 'Did this mum of yours come and claim you?'

'No, I got adopted.'

'Hmmm,' says Tanya, sighing. 'My little sister's adopted. It's easier when you're little and cute.'

'Do you still get to see her?'

'Nope. Well, not enough. They say it unsettles her. Of course it does. She misses me like crazy. And I miss her.'

'We know it's really hard on you, Tanya,' says Pat, putting her arm round her. Tanya shrugs the arm away.

'I'm OK. No need to feel sorry for me. And I've got Mandy now. She's this little kid over the road. She's like a little sister, sort of. You got any sisters, April? Adopted ones?'

I shake my head.

5

There were just the three of us. They adopted me, Janet and Daniel Johnson. They gave me my name, Johnson. They wanted to give me a new first name too. Danielle, after my new dad. But I wouldn't answer, wouldn't even look up, no matter how many times they said it. They told me this as I got older, laughing, but you could tell it still bugged them a bit.

'You were really only a baby too – and a

good little girl in most other respects,' said Mummy.

'You just didn't want to be a daddy's girl,' said Daddy, pulling one of my plaits a little too hard.

Too right I didn't. Not *his* girl. Or hers either, come to that.

Is that really true? Maybe I loved them then. I still miss *her* sometimes.

Tanya is watching me.

'Come up to my room for a bit, April,' she says. 'I got these incredible new shoes on Saturday. You've got to see them.'

'Yes, that money was supposed to be for *school* clothes,' says Pat, stirring the mince a little too vigorously. 'As if you could ever get away with wearing those heels to school.'

'Well, I haven't *got* a school yet, so what's the point wasting money on boring kid's stuff?' says Tanya. 'Come on, April.'

She props Ricky on the floor, pops his dummy in his mouth, and prods me upstairs.

Tanya obviously shares her room with one of the babies. It's lilac and fluffy, with a lamb mobile and a Little Bo Peep lamp. I wonder if this was ever my room? Did I ever sleep in that battered old cot in the comer?

Tanya sees me looking and raises her eyebrows.

'Yeah, it's too gruesome, this dinky room. Wait till I get my own place. I've got it all sussed out. I want one of those converted warehouse lofts, all polished wood and white rugs, matt black furniture, kind of minimal chic.'

'It sounds great,' I say politely, as if it actually exists.

'Yeah,' says Tanya, sighing. Her eyes meet mine.

'As if!'

I laugh sympathetically.

'Still, I could get lucky. There's no chance of me being adopted like my little sister, I'm too old for that lark now, but give me another couple of years and I might meet some rich guy who'll want to set me up somewhere stylish. Then my sister can come and live with me – or maybe my friend Mandy across the road. We play these games together, her and me. Pretend games. Don't laugh.'

'I play pretend games too sometimes.'

'So, your new mum and dad? The ones that adopted you? Something tells me it's not all Happy Families,' says Tanya.

'You got it. Well, we're not any kind of family any more,' I say, leaning against the little cot. I fiddle with the bars, lowering them so I can perch on the edge. I fight a mad desire to scrunch up really small and curl up in the cot myself. I smooth the Thomas the Tank Engine quilt.

'The new mum didn't dump you in a dustbin too, did she?' says Tanya.

'No. She was OK, I suppose,' I say, pleating the quilt. Thomas the Tank Engine is concertinaed up tight.

'Was?' says Tanya. She's changed her tone. She perches beside me. 'Is she dead?

'Mmm.'

'What, she got cancer or something?'

'No, she . . .'

'I get it,' Tanya says softly. 'Yeah, *my* mum topped herself.'

Neither of us say anything for a minute. I don't have to pretend with Tanya. I can really talk to her. But there are some things you can't ever tell.

'And your dad?' Tanya says eventually.

'Him!'

'Ah,' says Tanya. 'So, who are you with now? You're not in a Children's Home, are you?'

'I was for a while. I've lived all over. But I've got this new foster mother, Marion. She's OK. But she's not like a real mum.' I pause, smoothing the quilt out again. Thomas the Tank Engine looks as if he's been in a bad train crash.

'Is that why you came to take a deck at Pat?' Tanya asks.

'I thought – oh, it's so daft, I was just a baby, but I wondered if I'd remember her. What's she like, Tanya? She seems . . . nice.'

'She *is* nice, I suppose. Well, she nags a bit, but then that's a mumsie thing, isn't it? She's good with all the babies. She never gets rattled even when they're yelling fit to bust, and she never really loses her rag with me – but maybe that's because she doesn't really care, like. I'm just this dodgy girl who's been foisted on her, like a visitor. She does her best to make me feel welcome but when I go she won't miss me.'

I don't suppose she missed me either. I was here eleven months but I wasn't ever *her* baby. I was just one of many to be fed and changed and cared for.

'Where are you going then, Tanya?'

She shrugs. 'Don't ask me. This is just a temporary placement till they can find somewhere else.' She nibbles a nail, looking at me sideways. 'This Marion — she doesn't specialize in teenagers, does she?'

'Not really. I think I'm just a special case because she knew me before. But I suppose I could ask her—'

'No, no, I'm OK here for now. And I want to stay pals with Mandy. Like I said, we're like sisters.'

'*Her* mum couldn't foster you?'

Tanya grins. 'I don't think her mum can stick me. I'm a bad influence on her precious little diddums.'

'They said I was a bad influence once.'

'You!' Tanya cracks up laughing. 'You're like Goody Goody Two Shoes.'

I grin too. 'That's all part of the act. Hey, where are *your* shoes then?'

'Oh, right.' Tanya shows off the most amazing shiny mock-croc pink high heels.

'Wow! Yeah, just the thing for school!' I say, as Tanya struts around.

'Can I try them on?'

'Sure.'

I have a go, stepping out gingerly. I catch sight of myself in the wardrobe mirror and get the giggles.

'It's not fair. They look great on you but I just look daft.'

'No, you look fine – though try not to let your bum stick out like that. Sway your hips.'

'I haven't *got* any hips,' I say, tottering around.

'Try these on. They're not quite so high,' says Tanya, finding me an electric blue pair of wedges. 'Yeah, they've got a strap see, so you can keep them on easier. And look, they go great with this little denim skirt. Try it and see. It's designer, look.' She shows off the label.

'Did Pat buy it for you?'

'You're joking! No, she doesn't know I've got half this stuff.'

I remember the older kids at Sunnybank and the way they supplemented their wardrobes. 'Did you nick it?'

'Of course not,' says Tanya, but then she winks. 'One or two little bits might just have fallen into my bag, right? You're not shocked, are you?'

I shake my head, trying to look cool.

Tanya laughs. 'Do you nick stuff too, April?'

I shrug. I never *wanted* to nick anything. Not so much as a bar of chocolate from the sweet shop. Not even a chip off someone else's plate. But I got forced into doing stuff. I don't care if Tanya is a thief. It's like her Pat says. We shouldn't pass judgement.

Well, I can just imagine what Marion would say on that one.

Marion.

I wonder what happens when you don't turn up at school They wouldn't ring Marion, would they? No, of course not. The teachers probably won't even notice I'm not there.

Cathy and Hannah will be wondering about me though. Especially as it's my birthday. They might ring home at lunchtime.

I'll go now.

But I don't go. I stay in Tanya's bedroom, trying on half her clothes. They look totally weird on me. I look such a baby still. Even Tanya's crop tops hang loose and I haven't got any boobs to fill out her tube.

'Perhaps you need a spot of make-up?' Tanya suggested.

So I slap it on and then fix my hair so it's piled up on top, with little strands falling round my outlined eyes. I stuff a couple of socks inside a bra, slip on the killer pink heels and then pose with one hand on my hip.

I still look about ten years old.

'Maybe you're not up for a night's clubbing just yet,' says Tanya.

'Oh well. Marion wouldn't let me anyway,' I say, wiping most of the make-up off.

'And you do what she says?'

'Some of the time. She's a bit old-fashioned. Like out of the Ark. She didn't half create when I had my ears pierced. But she gave me special earrings for my birthday,' I say guiltily.

'Oh yeah, I forgot it was your birthday.' Tanya scrabbles in her make-up bag. 'Where's that glitter stuff? Aha!' She finds a special little tube from Claire's Accessories. 'Here. I've only used a little bit. Happy Birthday!'

'Are you sure? Thank you!'

'Course I'm sure, silly. Here, I'll put it on for you.'

I parade around in Tanya's clothes, my cheeks sparkling – and then I sigh and stick my school uniform back on. 'I'd better be going.'

'You keep saying that. Stay for lunch. Go on.'

So I sit down at the kitchen table with Tanya and Pat and the three little boys all strapped into their highchairs. The two toddlers ladle their own mince into their mouths (and laps) while Pat scoops spoonfuls of mince into Ricky's gaping mouth. She must have spooned meals into me too. My mouth opens now like a baby bird. I imagine her wiping the slurp off my chin and in and out of my clasped fingers, then whisking me off to change my nappy and tuck me up into my cot.

'Yes poppet, din dins, yum yum, now time for beddy-byes,' she said to me too. I'd burble back to her, repeating sounds. I expect I said my first word to her. But it wouldn't have been 'Mum'.

She sat me up, she lay me down, she tossed me in the air. She saw me crawl across the carpet and she kissed me better when I bumped my head. She let me play drums on her saucepans, she let me lick the honey spoon, she played round and round the garden in my palm and tickled me until I squealed. Maybe she acted just like a mum but when I went away she forgot all about me.

Maybe my *real* mum has forgotten about me too.

Mummy would have remembered.

I'd better remember her.

6

I say goodbye to Pat after lunch. She gives me a nod and a smile, busy with one of the little boys who's smeared custard into his curls. She doesn't put her arms round me or kiss me.

Tanya gives me a hug.

'Keep in touch, Dustbin Baby,' she says. 'What's your mobile number, eh?'

'I haven't got one,' I say, sighing. 'Marion

won't let me. She fusses that they give you brain cancer and says they're a social nuisance. I thought she might just give me one for my birthday, even so – but she didn't.'

'Well, here's mine,' Tanya says pityingly, handing me a proper printed card with her name and a computer-designed girl with orange hair and the message KEEP IN TOUCH. It's actually wrongly spelt TUTCH but I wouldn't point this out for the world.

She whips out a fluffy pink personal organizer and writes down Marion's phone number with *My mate Ayprel* next to it.

I feel thrilled that we are mates. We hug again and then I set off, walking as if I know where I'm going.

Well, I do know. I'm just not very clear how to get there. I don't fancy trying another taxi. I walk towards the town centre and see the sign to the railway station. I get a Travelcard to London and then curl up in a corner of the carriage, staring out the window at all the back gardens, thinking about Mummy.

She adopted me. I can remember the first time she picked me up. Lavender. Soft lavender talc and soft lavender blouse, slippery to the touch.

I'm imagining it. I can't *really* remember being one year old. It's just they told me so many times. Though I can close my eyes and smell her talc and feel her silky blouse. I see a pale purple blur whenever I think of her.

I gave her a cake of Yardley's lavender soap and a tin of lavender talcum every birthday and Christmas. She always cried and said, 'Oh April, darling, what a lovely surprise!' though they were the most predictable presents ever and she'd been watching out of the corner of her eye while he nudged me to the right corner of Boots to help me purchase them.

I called him Daddy, I called her Mummy. They called me Danielle for the first few months, tried a few variations – Dannie, Ella – but by the time I was eighteen months and anyone asked my name I'd say April.

Could I, really? I think that's what they said. One of Mummy's stories. Maybe she made half of it up. I've made up heaps myself and now I can't remember what's real. They don't seem real. Neither do I. Maybe that's why I hung on to the name April. It made me feel myself.

So my name stayed April and Mummy and Daddy had to like it or lump it. There were lots of lumps in our relationship.

Mummy wasn't very good at holding me. I was always small and slight but I was a very squirmy little girl and I suppose she was terrified of dropping me. She strapped me in a chair to feed me. She anchored me in a corner of the bath with a giant inflatable seahorse. She buckled me into my buggy on outings. She caged me in my cot at nights. She never hugged me tight or whirled me around or lumped me about on her hip. She'd sit me on her lap occasionally when I cried but she was as tense as a spring underneath her soft slippery skirt, and I soon slid off of my own accord.

Daddy was into cuddles in a big way but I wasn't sure I was keen on them from him. He loved playing bears with me, down on all fours and growling fit to bust. He was like a bear in real life. He could be fun, he could be friendly, but he could suddenly lose his temper and roar. I felt he could kill me with one swat. He even looked like a bear, with thick brown fuzzy curls and a big beard and hair all over his body, even on his back and shoulders. His legs were dark with it, leaving his feet as pale as plaice, though the hair sprouted again on top of his toes. He seemed proud of his hairiness, flaunting himself in brief trunks whenever we went to the beach.

Mummy wore a swimming costume then, but with a sarong around her waist and a cardi knotted over her shoulders. I was very pale so she oiled me with sunscreen until I was as greasy as a bag of chips, and made me pull on longsleeved T-shirts and a sunhat so big it rested on my nose.

I wasn't allowed ice-cream because Mummy didn't want me to eat frozen germs. Hot dogs and hamburgers were forbidden when we went to funfairs because Mummy was wary of warmed-up germs too. She held me out at arm's length over public lavatories so lurking germs had no chance of leaping up my bottom.

Daddy did things differently. He bought me knickerbocker glories with whipped cream and crimson cherries. He took me on every ride in the funfair, even the big wheel, though my stomach turned over and then inside out and I was sick all the way down to the ground and some poor soul got horribly splattered. Daddy always roared with laughter when he told this tale. He called it his sick sick joke. Mummy always shuddered. She had a weak stomach and when I was sick or worse at home she heaved as she cleared it up, putting on a brand new pair of pink Marigold gloves each time and throwing them away in fastened plastic bags afterwards.

I wondered if she felt she'd made a mistake adopting me. Maybe she secretly fancied fastening me into a big plastic bag and dumping me back in the dustbin where I belonged. Maybe I was wrong. She didn't hug me tight but every night after she'd kissed the space above my cheek she'd whisper into the darkness, 'I love you very much, April. You've changed our whole lives. You've made us so happy.'

Mummy and Daddy didn't *seem* happy. Mummy often sighed to herself, her face pained, her shoulders drooping. Sometimes she sighed so loudly she put her hand over her mouth apologetically, as if she were suffering from indigestion.

Daddy suffered from real indigestion, forever burping and farting; Mummy ignored these eruptions and expected me to do the same. Daddy was often sick too. I thought he might be ill but as I got older I realized this only happened when he came home late. Daddy didn't drink much at home but he sank pint after pint down at the pub. That was why he smelt so strange.

Mummy didn't nag him about it but she couldn't stop her sighs. Daddy started stopping out half the night.

I couldn't understand why Mummy minded so. I liked it with Daddy out the way. I wanted Mummy all to myself. I wanted her to help me dress my Barbie dolls, to draw little girls and kittens and butterflies with my crayons, to thread red and green glass beads so I could wear ruby necklaces and emerald bracelets.

Sometimes she did her best and put Barbie in her party dress and crayoned a cat family and decked me in jewellery. Other times she'd just sit sighing, and when she heard the door at last she'd jump up so suddenly that Barbie would land on her head and crayons and beads rolled over the carpet.

One morning Daddy wasn't back at breakfast and Mummy didn't eat but drank cups of tea all day, her spoon going clink, clink, clink as she stirred. Daddy came home from work at his normal time, but he had a big bunch of red roses. He pressed them into Mummy's arms. She held them loosely, not responding. He plucked a single rose from the bunch, stuck the stem sideways into his mouth, clasped Mummy in his arms and started a wild tango, stepping up and down the hall and bending Mummy backwards. She protested but then started giggling helplessly. Daddy grinned too, and the rose fell from his mouth and got trampled into the carpet. Mummy didn't rush for the vacuum. She stayed in Daddy's arms, smiling.

I glared at her.

'Ooh, look at April!' said Daddy. 'Somebody's gone green-eyed all of a sudden.'

He tried to get me to dance with him but I sat in the corner of the hall and sucked my thumb. I wasn't the least bit jealous. I didn't want to dance with Daddy. I was furious that Mummy could be so easily won over.

I suppose she adored him. That was why she put up with so much. She must have held her tongue when they were being grilled about adopting me. They had to present themselves as the perfect couple. Maybe Daddy was perfect in Mummy's eyes. Though he couldn't give her children. That was why she was so keen to adopt me. She felt it was her best chance of hanging on to him. Give him his own little girl. Little Danielle. Only I wouldn't play the game properly so it didn't work.

Daddy stayed out again. And again and again. He came back with one more bunch of flowers. Then he came back drunk. Then he came back in a towering rage, shouting at Mummy, yelling at me, as if it was all our fault.

Then he didn't come back. Mummy waited all day. Another night. Then she rang the office. I don't know what he said to her.

I found her sitting on the carpet by the telephone table in the hall, her legs stuck out, as ungainly as my Barbie doll. Tears ran down her cheeks. She didn't try to mop them. She didn't even blow her nose though it was running right down to her lips. I hovered beside her, terrified.

'Mummy?' I leant against her, wanting her to put her arms round me. She didn't move so eventually I wound my arms round her neck instead. She didn't seem to notice.

'Mummy, please talk to me!'

She didn't respond, even when I shouted right in her ear. I wondered if she might be dead but she blinked every now and then, her lashes stuck together with tears.

'It's all right, Mummy, I'm here,' I said, but of course it wasn't all right.

She didn't care whether I was there or not. No, that's not true. She did care. She tried to look after me over the next few weeks. She didn't bother to wash herself and she pulled the same old jogging trousers and jerkin over her nightie when she trailed me to the Infants and back but she still supervised my bath every night and stuffed my arms down fresh blouse sleeves every day. She wasn't totally systematic. She remembered my school uniform but forgot my growing pile of grubby socks and underwear so that one day I had to go to school in Mummy's own large white nylon knickers, pulled up at the waist with a safety pin. It took me ages to get the pin undone in the dark lavatories and I wet myself a little but nobody found out. I tried washing the damp knickers at home with soap in the bathroom. This seemed to work so I washed all my own underwear and hung them all along the bath and over every tap. But I didn't rinse them through properly so they were stiff and uncomfortable and made me itch.

Mummy couldn't manage meals now. She didn't seem to eat at all, she just drank endless cups of tea, taking it black after we ran out of milk. I ate my breakfast cornflakes straight out of the packet. I ate a lot of school lunch because we were just using up all the tins of baked beans in the cupboard for tea. I had baked beans on toast, and then when we'd used all the bread in the freezer I simply had baked beans. When Mummy just sat and stared into space I ate the baked beans cold.

One teatime I couldn't get her to open the tin. I tried and tried with the tin opener but I couldn't work out how to do it and ended up cutting myself. It was only a tiny cut at the end of my thumb but it frightened me and I howled. Mummy burst into tears too and sobbed that she was sorry. She said she was a useless mother and an awful wife and it was no wonder he'd walked out on us. He was much better off without her and I'd be much better off without her too.

She said it over and over again, louder and louder, her pale face almost purple with emotion. I was so scared that I nodded, imagining she wanted me to agree with her.

7

I don't want to remember any more. I'll only start crying. It won't be April Showers, it will be April Downpour.

What am I doing here, snivelling in a corner of this dusty old train? I'm meant to be having a special day. It's my *birthday*. I don't want to be thinking about deathdays. It's weird – each year you pass the date of your own deathday and yet you obviously don't know it. Unless you choose it for yourself.

That's what she did. Mummy. They think I can't remember because I've never talked about it to anyone. Not the social workers. Not the child psychiatrist. Not even Marion. They think five is too young to remember which is mad because I know every detail of that day. I overheard one social worker say I must have blanked it out. I don't know how they think I can do that. Take a blackboard eraser and go swish, swish, swish across my brain and there it is, sponged clean, good as new, no memory of any messy suicide.

It must have been very messy. She cut her wrists in the bath. She didn't want me to see. She locked herself in the bathroom on Sunday night, after she'd phoned a woman down the road and asked her to take me to school in the morning because she wasn't feeling very well. It was a kind plan but I mucked it up.

I woke up early and needed to go to the bathroom – only of course it was locked. I twisted and turned the door knob. I knocked. I called. 'Mummy? Are you in there? *Mummy!*'

She wasn't in her bed. She wasn't drinking

tea in the kitchen. She had to be in the bathroom. I didn't panic too much at first. I was used to Mummy not answering when she was in a mood. Maybe she'd gone to sleep in the bath? She never seemed to go to bed at nights now which made her doze a lot during the day. I knocked again and again. I was worried I might wet myself so I padded downstairs, knock-kneed, and struggled with the bolt on the back door until I was able to let myself out into the garden. There was a dark toilet in a wooden shed at the back. I hated using it because I was frightened of spiders. They scuttled over my bare feet and made me squeal but I managed not to leap up mid-wee. I trailed back into the garden, wondering what to do next. I looked up and saw the bathroom window was open at the top.

'Mummy!' I called up. 'Mummy, please!'

She didn't call back. Mrs Stevenson next door peered out of her bedroom window. She and Mummy had once had words because of the Stevenson boy's loud music so I scuttled away like the spiders, scared she was going to tell me off.

'April! April, don't run away! I'm talking to you!'

I'd got to the back door but couldn't quite get inside.

'*April!*'

I turned round very reluctantly. Mrs Stevenson was leaning right out of her bedroom window. She was in her nightie. I could see a lot of pink bosom from my underneath angle.

'Why are you out in the garden at this time of the morning? Where's your mum?'

'In the bathroom,' I said, and I burst into tears.

I sobbed out a lot of stuff about locked doors. After a minute Mr Stevenson joined his wife at the window, his hair all sticking up sideways, wearing a vest instead of pyjamas. Mr Stevenson had a temper. I was scared he'd shout at me for waking him, but to my surprise they both came downstairs and out into *their* garden, and then Mr Stevenson fetched a ladder and tipped it over the fence and climbed over afterwards and propped it up against the back of the house, next to the bathroom window.

I was getting very agitated because I knew Mummy would be appalled if she saw Mr Stevenson's big red face suddenly looking at her. I begged Mr Stevenson not to, but he explained that Mummy might have fainted.

Mr Stevenson was the one who nearly fainted when he got to the top of his ladder and peered in.

He swayed for a moment and then climbed down again, his feet missing rungs so that he almost fell. When he got to the bottom he took several deep breaths, his hand clamped to his mouth. Little beads of sweat trickled down his forehead.

'Joe? You all right?' Mrs Stevenson called over the fence.

'Is it Mummy? What's the matter with Mummy?' I whispered.

He jumped, as if he'd forgotten all about me. He looked appalled.

'Where's your dad, April?'

'I don't know. I want Mummy!'

'Well . . . she's not very well,' he said. 'You'd better come into our house for a bit while I call some people to see to your mum.'

He took hold of my hand. His was damp and I didn't want to hold it. I didn't want to go off with him. I knew Mummy wouldn't like it. But I didn't seem to have any option. I had to do as I was told.

He passed me over the fence to Mrs Stevenson. I felt very undignified just in my nightie, worried that my bottom might show. She took me into her house. It had a funny smell of old cooking and it was very bright with orange walls and yellow kitchen units. I stood blinking at the oddness of being in a house exactly the same as mine but back to front and totally transformed. It was like being in a dream. I began to wonder if I could still be dreaming because everything was so bewilderingly strange. I wanted Mummy to come and wake me up.

But she was the one who was sleeping. That's what they said.

I was kept indoors with Mrs Stevenson while an ambulance and police cars drew up outside. There was enough thumping and carrying on to wake the dead. Only it didn't.

Mrs Stevenson kept glancing anxiously at

me. She wouldn't tell me what was going on. She tried to divert me by pouring me a big glass of milk. I wasn't very keen on milk now but didn't like to tell her in case she thought me rude.

'Drink it all up, dear,' she said, and so I did my best, though the milk smell turned my stomach and it tasted sour when I swallowed. I sipped and sipped and sipped until I felt so full of milk I expected it to slop straight out of my mouth and spout from each ear.

'That's it, dear, have some more,' she said, refilling my glass.

I was still sipping when the policewoman came to see me. She knelt down beside me.

'Hello, April,' she said. Her voice was odd. She didn't quite look me in the eye. My stomach clenched, the milk churning into rancid butter.

'I want Mummy,' I whispered.

The policewoman was blinking a lot. She patted my hands.

'I'm afraid Mummy's gone to sleep,' she said.

I was used to Mummy sleeping. 'You have

to keep shaking her and then she wakes up.'

'I'm afraid Mummy can't wake up now,' she said. 'She's going to stay asleep.'

'But she's in the bathroom! Has she gone to bed in the bath?'

They'd lifted her out of the bath and wrapped her up and removed her. There was no trace of her when they eventually let me back into the house. The policewoman helped me pack a small suitcase, telling me she was going to take me to a kind lady's house and she would look after me for a while. She probably had an Auntie Pat in mind.

But someone tracked down Daddy at his office and he suddenly burst into the house.

'Where's my poor little April?' he called, and he rushed into my room and swept me up into his arms, squeezing me tight. Too tight.

I was horribly, milkily sick all down the back of his suit.

8

I'm surprised Daddy didn't back off there and then the minute he'd sluiced off his suit. But he took me to his new flat. Was it his place – or hers? *She* was called Sylvia. There's some silly song that goes 'Who is Sylvia, what is she?' and Daddy kept singing it. I knew exactly who Sylvia was. She was Daddy's new girlfriend. I knew *what* she was too. She was wicked because she had enticed Daddy away from Mummy.

Maybe that's not fair. I don't know how they met or when they started their affair. I just knew that if Sylvia hadn't come on the scene Daddy might have stayed with Mummy so she wouldn't have slit her wrists.

I didn't see her, of course. Nobody told me what she'd done but I heard them whispering. I imagined Mummy and her lady's razor and her pale body and the crimson bathwater. It seemed clear that it had to be *their* fault, Daddy and Sylvia.

I had to stay with Sylvia while Daddy went to the funeral. I didn't properly understand what a funeral was so I didn't clamour to go. Daddy bought me a new Barbie doll and a big tub of wax crayons and coloured drawing paper and a pile of picture books but I didn't touch any of them. I asked for scissors and cut pictures out of magazines. Sylvia was into fashion in a big way so I carefully cut out long lanky models with skinny arms and legs, my tongue sticking out as I rounded each spiky wrist and bony ankle, occasionally performing unwitting amputations as I went.

Sylvia found me an old exercise book and a

stick of Pritt but I didn't want to make a scrapbook. I wanted to keep my paper girls free. They weren't called Naomi and Kate and Elle and Natasha. They were my girls now so I called them Rose and Violet and Daffodil and Bluebell. I weakened over the wax crayons and gave my girls' black-and-white high-fashion frocks bright red and purple and yellow and blue floral patterns to match their names.

'That's this month's *Vogue*,' Sylvia said irritably, but most of the time we didn't speak. She fixed me lunch and then watched me warily. Perhaps she'd been the one who had to wash the sick out of the suit. My peanut-butter sandwich and Ribena stayed in my stomach so she relaxed and switched on the television. And then at long last Daddy came back.

'What did Mummy look like?' I asked.

Daddy flinched, not knowing what to say. I wasn't being deliberately awkward. I didn't understand that Mummy was dead – and now indeed buried. I'd been told she was asleep and that she wasn't coming back home but I'd be able to meet up with her again in Heaven. Mummy had read me fairy tales so I imagined her sleeping in a castle surrounded by briars in some distant holiday resort called Heaven.

Daddy didn't answer. He had a lot of whispered discussions with Sylvia. Sometimes they got angry and forgot to whisper. Then they made up passionately and I'd come across them in an unpleasant embrace. I tried hard not to take any notice. I clutched my crumpled paper friends in my hands and in my head I played Big Girls, going out dancing with Rose and Violet and Daffodil and Bluebell.

I couldn't dance for ever. I cried at night when I was supposed to be sleeping on Sylvia's sofa. I cried during the day too, in the toilets at school, though I always blew my nose and scrubbed my face with crackly paper before I sidled out of the cubicle.

People tiptoed round me at school. I think the other children had been warned not to mention my mother. They played safe and didn't talk to me at all, not even my best friend Betsy. She acted as if maternal suicide was catching. We still had to sit next to each other but she edged as far away as possible and charged out every playtime so as not to get stuck with me. She started going round with another little girl called Charmaine. They circled the playground arm in arm whispering secrets. I tried bribing Betsy back by giving her my new Barbie doll but she said witheringly that dolls were for babies – though I knew she had a big girly gang of Barbies back at home because I'd played with them when I went to tea at her house.

I couldn't ask her back to our house any more because we didn't live in it.

But then we did. Daddy moved us back – and Sylvia came too.

'But it's Mummy's house!' I said. 'She won't let Sylvia in.'

'Don't be silly, April. You know Mummy's passed away. It's my house and so of course I'm going to live in it. With Sylvia. She's your new mummy.'

I wasn't having it. Sylvia didn't seem keen on the idea either.

'I hate this house. I hate the way everyone

round here looks at me,' she shouted. 'I don't want to live here. I don't want to look after your creepy little kid. I want to have fun! I'm out of here.'

So she went. So then there was just Daddy and me. He didn't know what to do with me. He asked Mrs Stevenson if she could fetch me from school and look after me till he got home from work. Mrs Stevenson made it plain that she didn't want to, except in emergencies. I begged Daddy to ask Betsy's mum, seeing it as a brilliant way of making Betsy be friends again, but she turned me down too, saying she didn't want the responsibility.

'One well-behaved quiet little girl?' said Daddy impatiently.

I tried hard to be well-behaved around Daddy then because he was very bad-tempered, and I was very, very quiet in the real world. Inside my head I shouted all sorts of stuff with Rose and Violet and Daffodil and Bluebell. We played all day and danced all night. We could look after ourselves. We didn't need mothers or fathers.

Daddy employed an old lady to ferry me

backwards and forwards. She came into our house and settled herself down in front of the television as if it was her place. I couldn't bear her to sit in Mummy's chair. I didn't want her big bottom squashing Mummy's pale lilac cushions. I raced to sit on Mummy's chair myself and wouldn't get up when she asked me. She smacked me hard on the back of my skinny legs. I kicked her. She walked out there and then.

So Daddy employed a young woman student instead. Jennifer. She was pink and plump and gentle and showed me how to paste my frail paper girls onto cardboard cornflake packets so they became reassuringly sturdy. I liked Jennifer a lot. Unfortunately Daddy did too. She showed him a lot more than cardboard cut-outs. Jennifer moved in. She didn't just commandeer Mummy's chair. She moved in on Mummy's bed.

I wasn't allowed into the bedroom now. I slumped outside in the hall, feeling lonely. For once Rose and Violet and Bluebell and Daffodil failed to keep me company.

I went into the bathroom and stared where the bath had been. Daddy had changed it into a shower stall because Sylvia said the bath gave her the creeps. It was one change too many. I wanted the bath back. I wanted to lie down in it and pretend I was cuddled up to Mummy. I wanted to prise open her eyelids so she would stay awake for ever.

I wanted her so badly.

I started whispering her name. The whispers got louder and louder until I was screaming. There was a lot of knocking at the door. I thought I'd locked it but Daddy's full weight made the lock burst open and then there were fingers digging into my shoulders and I was lifted off the floor and shaken so that my head jerked backwards and forwards and the bathroom became a fairground ride.

Daddy's voice bellowed, 'STOP THAT SCREAMING!' I couldn't stop because he was scaring me so. I wouldn't stop for Jennifer. I wouldn't stop for Mrs Stevenson who came rushing around to see if I was being murdered. I screamed until my throat was raw. Daddy had to send for the doctor who stuck a needle in my bottom. He said it would send me to sleep which made me scream all the more.

The doctor said I was suffering from 'Nervous Reaction'. It wasn't surprising, given the circumstances. He said I just needed lots of love and reassurance.

I suppose Daddy tried. For a day or two. 'Don't look so droopy, April. Daddy's here. Daddy loves you. Come on, how about a smile? Am I going to have to tickle you? Tickle, tickle, tickle,' and his hard fingertips would poke under my chin or into my armpit until Daddy interpreted my grimace as a grin.

Most of the time he let me mope. I was in trouble at school. I put my head down on my desk and shut my eyes. The teacher asked Daddy if I was getting enough sleep at night. He said I was getting too much, if anything. I wasn't always waking up in time to run to the bathroom. There were always damp sheets flapping in the back garden now. Daddy got angry and called me a baby. Jennifer said it wasn't really my fault and I couldn't help being nervy, like my mother.

'She wasn't her *real* mother,' said Daddy.

He wasn't my real father and I'm glad, glad, glad there isn't a drop of his blood in my body. He was glad too, because when he'd eventually had enough of me – only months after Mummy died – he could shove me straight back to the social workers. Into Care.

Only it seemed that no one really cared for me now.

I wonder if Mummy would have given up on me too. I've tried so hard but I can't *really* remember her. She's just a feeling, a faint smell of lavender, a sad sigh.

I think I still need to see her though. I know where she is.

9

The Greenwood Cemetery. It was written in my records. I imagined it was a real green wood, a gothic fairytale cemetery, tall yews and ivy and marble angels, but Greenwood is a London suburb and the cemetery is a long hike up a busy dual carriageway. I get to the gates at last and look for someone to give me directions. There's no one around.

I don't like it being so empty. I wish I had someone with me. I really want to run right back to the station – but I can't give up now.

I could wait and ask Marion . . .

No. I'm here. It's OK. I'm not a little kid. I don't believe in ghosts even though I'm so haunted by the past.

I set off, selecting a path at random. There are a few angels, but their wings are broken and some have their heads knocked right off. I pat a pair of little mossy feet, stroke a marble robe, hold hands with a tiny cherub without a nose. It seems so shocking that no-one tends these graves any more. Vandals whack at them with baseball bats, thinking it's a right laugh. I want to cry even though the people in the graves have long ago crumpled into dust. A hundred years or more. Too long ago for Mummy.

I try another path, a bit scared of getting lost. My footsteps crunch on the gravel. I stop every now and then, wondering if I can hear someone else. I stop and peer round. The new leaves on the trees rustle, branches bobbing up and down. There are so many places someone could be hiding. Boys with bats, vagrants, junkies . . .

I'm being silly. There's no one here. The footsteps I keep hearing are my own. I take a deep breath and walk on through the Victorian graves, reaching the classier end of the cemetery, all plinths and columns and little houses for the dead. I wonder what it's like to trace your family way back, to finger the gold lettering and find your great-great-great-great grandmother. My great-great-great-great grandmother could have been a posh old lady in a silk crinoline or a wretched old beggar-woman in rags. I'll never know.

I hurry past, marching towards the regimented rows of recent gravestones, wincing at freshly dug mounds heaped with wreaths. I walk up one row and down the next, wishing the dead could be conveniently rearranged in alphabetical order. Maybe Mummy's grave isn't properly marked anyway. I don't think Daddy would have wanted to fork out on a gravestone. And how would he have it engraved? *Only sleeping? Much loved wife of Daniel, deeply mourned almost-mother of April?*

I trek backwards and forwards, my eyes watering in the brisk wind. I'm never going to find her. I don't need to see the exact spot. It's better to think of her the way I used to, sleeping like Snow White in the green wood of my imagination . . .

There she is! JANET JOHNSON. Bright gold lettering on shiny black stone – much too garish for Mummy. And there's a *photo*, a heart shape behind glass. I go closer, my heart beating.

It's not her.

It has to be her.

It could be a different Janet Johnson, it's a common enough name – though the dates are right. It *is* her.

She looks young. She's wearing some very fancy white bow in her hair. No, you fool, it's a bride's veil. It's a wedding-day photo. Typical Daddy – he'd insist the day she married him had to be the happiest day of her life. Maybe it was. She looks radiant. It's the word you always use about brides, but she truly looks lit up from within, light shining out of her eyes, her mouth open, showing her gleaming teeth.

She never looked like that when I knew her.

The light had been switched off. Poor Mummy.

I wish I could remember her properly. I wonder if she really loved me. Not the way she loved Daddy, but in a warm, soft, motherly way. Or was I always the odd little dustbin baby who never quite scrubbed up sweet enough?

I'm crying. I fumble in my schoolbag for a tissue.

'What's the matter then, love?'

I freeze.

A man dodges through the graves towards me – a man with wild hair and dirty clothes, clutching a bottle in his hand. I look round. No one else. Just him and me. And I'm a long, long way away from the cemetery gates.

I turn sharply and start walking away.

'Hey! Don't ignore me! I'm trying to be *helpful*. Want a hankie, eh?' He pulls out a filthy rag from his trouser pocket and waves it at me.

Is he just being kind? He doesn't look it. I shake my head and give him a quick, scared smile.

'Thank you – but I'm OK. Well, I've got to go now. Goodbye.'

'Don't go! I want to talk. What you crying for, eh? Want a drink? It'll make you feel better, darling.'

'No. Really.'

'Suit yourself. All the more for me.' He tips the bottle and drinks.

I walk on but he walks with me, lurching a little.

'Someone die then?' he asks.

'Yes. It's . . . my mother and – and my father's just over there.' I gesture vaguely beyond the graves. 'I'm going to catch up with him now. Goodbye.'

I run for it. I don't think he believes me. He calls after me but I don't stop. I hear his footsteps and I clench my fists and run harder, as fast as I can, my schoolbag banging against my hip. I run and run and run, twisting my ankle on tufts of grass, staggering as I zig-zag through gravestones, on and on, wondering if

I'm really going in the right direction. Maybe he's catching me up, his grimy hands reaching out to grab me but there's the arch of the cemetery gates, I'm nearly there! I rush towards them, through, out by the main road, cars whizzing past.

I lean against the stone wall, gasping for breath. I wait, ready to scream for help if I see him staggering towards me. But he doesn't come. He's given up, still somewhere in the cemetery. When my heart slows I walk on shakily, still sick and scared, but feeling a little safer now.

I don't know whether I should tell anyone. I'm not sure he really did anything to me. Maybe he really meant well – but it would have been crazy to wait to find out. I hated the way he was looking at me. I couldn't stand him calling me 'love' and 'darling'.

I think about my mother, my real mother, not poor Mummy neatly tucked up under her shiny black slab. Maybe my mother was attacked by some hateful drunken stranger? Maybe that's why she couldn't bear to keep me?

I don't know where I'm going now. The cars roar past, disorientating me. I keep looking back just in case the wild man follows me. I don't know what I'm doing here. It's like a dream. Nothing seems real any more.

But then I'm used to that.

10

I stopped feeling real after Mummy died and Daddy got shot of me. I felt as papery and easily crumpled as Daffodil and Bluebell and Rose and Violet. I had two foster mothers in quick succession. I read it in my notes.

The first one was another short-term specialist like Auntie Pat. I think I can remember my sixth birthday there. I left the white-icing rosebuds from my birthday cake because they looked so pretty but someone took my plate away before I could save them.

Then I went to live with Maureen and Peter. Their friends all called them Big Mo and Little Pete. Did we call them that too? Probably not. I think we just called them Mum and Dad. We were their foster children and there were a lot of us. Some came for a few days, some a few years. Some lived there for ever.

I asked Big Mo if I was going to live there for ever. 'Probably, little sweetiepops,' she said, and then she charged off to separate two of the big boys who were fighting and unhook one of the little boys who'd wound himself round and round in the long living-room curtains.

That was the way it was. You never got the chance to have a proper talk. There was never time for her to stop and give you a cuddle. I didn't really want one anyway. Big Mo was a good kindhearted woman but I didn't like the way she looked. She *was* Big – probably only a bit taller than average but she seemed to tower ten metres in the air when I was little and she seemed ten metres *wide* too. Big Mo was like a mountain range, vast slopes of bosom and belly and bottom. She wore great patterned sack dresses, bright red jersey in the winter and pink floral print in the summer. She never wore tights even in the coldest spells so her legs were mottled red and pink too. Sometimes when she sat on the battered sofa you got a glimpse of her awesome knickers. Everyone used to giggle uncontrollably when she pulled her clean pairs out the washing machine. Big Mo didn't seem to mind. When she was in a good mood she'd wave her knickers in the air like flags and we'd all fall about.

Little Pete wasn't *that* little, just normal size, but he looked like one of us kids beside Big Mo. He behaved like a kid in lots of ways too, down on his bands and knees making mudpies with the little ones and fixing the bikes and chatting fanatically about football with the big ones. He even had a go on their scooters. Big Mo got very irritated when he fell off and sprained his wrist and couldn't help her around the house for a week. Little Pete winked at the boys happily and they guffawed.

I didn't fit in. They were mostly boys there and I was an exceptionally girly girl at that stage because of the way Mummy had brought me up. I liked to keep my dinky little dresses clean. Big Mo bought me a pair of dungarees with an embroidered bear on the pocket.

'There now, sweetiepops, you can run riot in your dungies. It doesn't matter a bit if you get them dirty,' said Big Mo.

But I didn't want to get them dirty. I sat crosslegged in a corner, head bent, chatting to the teddy bear. I pretended he was a real bear cub called Cuddly, and Bluebell, Daffodil, Violet and Rose took turns looking after him, feeding him honey and brushing his fur and taking him for walks on a silver chain lead.

'That little kid April is a right nutter! Always talking to herself. Whisper, whisper, whisper. What a little weirdo!' said the boys. Sometimes they barged into me on purpose when they were playing football. Once they tipped me upside down and my flower girls got scattered and Daffodil got trodden on, mud all over her yellow dress, and Rose lost a leg and had to make do with a crayoned pink prosthesis for the rest of her days.

I got teased when I tried to talk to the boys. I didn't understand about accents. I just knew I talked differently from the others. I suppose I talked like Mummy. I hadn't realized it before but this niminy-piminy way of talking seriously annoyed everyone. Even the word 'Mummy', which I called Big Mo once by mistake, sent everyone into hoots of laughter. I was mocked for days. The boys called me Posh-Nob and Swanky-Pants.

There was only one other girl at first and she sometimes copied the boys but she didn't mean to be nasty. Esme cheerfully copied everyone. She was much older than me, nearly grown-up, but she had Down's syndrome so she stayed like a little girl in lots of ways. I could already read but Esme couldn't get the hang of it, so I sometimes read her stories. Sometimes I made up my own stories for her, telling her my flower girls' current adventures. Esme was enchanted. She kept asking me where I got my stories *from*, not understanding they came out of my own head.

'The stories are in here,' I said.

'Show me!' said Esme, hooking my hair behind my ear and peering hard as if she could see right inside.

She liked my long hair, running her podgy fingers through it like a clumsy comb. Esme's own hair was cut short. It hung limp and brown either side of her flat face. I wondered if she knew she wasn't pretty. Out of earshot of Big Mo some of the boys called her nasty names but she didn't seem to take it to heart.

We played together a lot. I sometimes stopped talking in my own voice and copied Esme, using her easy short sentences. I spoke like this at my new school too and my teacher had a word with Big Mo.

I don't know whether it was because they were worried about me and my development but in a matter of weeks Big Mo and Little Pete started fostering another girl.

'She's called Pearl. She's a couple of years

older than you, April, and seems a little sweetheart in spite of everything. She's had a very bad time too, poor little pet. I think she'll be a good friend for you,' said Big Mo.

'I've got a friend,' I mumbled, but they didn't seem to count Esme, and they didn't know about Bluebell, Violet, Daffodil and limping Rose.

Pearl was supposed to be my friend now. She had black hair, big blue eyes and pearly teeth to match her name, the biggest whitest teeth I'd ever seen – all the better to bite me. She did too – but when Big Mo spotted the ring of purple toothmarks on my arm I said I'd bitten myself. I knew if I told on Pearl she'd inflict far more damage when we were alone together.

My heart still thuds when I think about her. Pearl was far, far more scary than any drunk in the cemetery.

Big Mo took Pearl and Esme and me out on Saturdays. We went to a film once, *Beauty and the Beast*. Esme loved the talking teapot and screamed with laughter every time it was on the screen. I didn't laugh. I didn't cry either – though Pearl wrenched my fingers backward in the dark and spat in my ice-cream tub. Big Mo thought we were holding hands and sharing ice-cream. Everyone thought Pearl and I were the best of friends.

I thought I was safe at school because Pearl should have been two years above me, but she'd missed out on so much schooling in the past she hadn't yet learnt to read so they put her back a couple of years. Into my class. They moved the little boy beside me so that Pearl could sit next to me, 'seeing as you two girls are such special friends'.

I tried to run away from Pearl at playtime but she could run much faster than me. She'd whack me hard with her book.

'You're supposed to help with my reading, April. Come on, get cracking, or I'll tell on you.'

I had to sit down beside her and open up the book and point to all the words about Freddy and his teddy. Pearl read along as I pointed, but she whispered her own words. She might not have been able to read conventionally but she could certainly read me.

'There was a stupid, spotty, smelly girl called April and no one liked her, not even her own mum and dad, so they dumped her, ha ha, what do you expect. This daft, fat lady said, "Oooh, never mind, April, little diddums, we will make Pearl be your friend." Do you think Pearl will be April's friend?' She said it as if she was still reading. She dug me viciously with her elbow. 'Oi, dumbo, I'm talking to you. Am I your friend? *Am I?*'

'No! Yes! I don't know,' I said helplessly.

'Can't you make up your mind, stupid? Well, I'll make it up for you. If you don't want to be my friend that means you're my deadly enemy.'

School was bad enough but Pearl was worse at home. I'd start to feel sick every evening when it got near bathtime. There were so many of us needing baths every day that Big Mo thought it would be fun for us girls to have our bath together.

I tried to hide but it was no use.

'Found you!' said Big Mo, and she'd haul me out from under the bed and give me a little shake. 'You're as bad as the boys,

sweetiepops. They don't like baths either. But you want to be a nice clean girl, don't you? Come on now. Pearl's already in the tub. She's squirting bubbles everywhere, bless her.'

I begged to have a bath with Esme instead.

'No, dearie. Esme's quite the little lady now in lots of ways. She needs her privacy. You pop in the tub with Pearl.'

Big Mo effortlessly held me up with her giant arms, suddenly squinting at me. 'What's up, eh? You and Pearl haven't had a little tiff, have you?'

I shook my head. 'A little tiff' implied an argument. I didn't dare disagree with Pearl.

I had to share the bath with her. When Big Mo was in the room with us Pearl couldn't go too far, though she'd pinch me under the bubbles and run her sharp toenails down my skinny legs. But when Big Mo went out the room to fetch some clean towels from the airer in the kitchen Pearl would play her favourite game. Mermaids.

'What do mermaids do, April?' she'd whisper, sitting really close to me, her teeth gleaming. Soapsuds glistened on her pale arms. Her wet black hair lay flat against her head, shiny like a Dutch doll.

'I'm talking to you, April. Can't you hear me? Haven't you got any ears?' She yanked a lock of my hair to one side and jabbed her finger right into my ear, making it ring.

'I – I don't know what mermaids do,' I stammered that first time.

'And you're such a clever-clogs too! Well, dopey, drippy April, mermaids have got long fishy tails so they can – what?'

I swallowed, trying to edge away from her until the hard enamel of the bath bit into my back.

'Answer me! Maybe you haven't got a tongue, is that it?' Her fingers scrabbled at my bottom lip until it opened. 'No, yuck, there it is, waggling away at me. So make it work. Tell me why mermaids have tails, April.'

'So they can swim,' I whispered.

'Hurray! She's got it! Top of the class! *Soooo* – swim!'

She suddenly seized me by both ankles and tugged hard. I shot forward and my head went back, under the water. I tried to struggle up, but Pearl's hands were hard on my chest, pressing me back. My legs kicked at her feebly but I couldn't see what I was doing. I had a terrible roaring in my head as if the water was whirling through my ears. I knew she was drowning me and in amongst the pain and the panic I had a moment of triumph – at *last* Pearl would get into trouble. But then her hands were suddenly under my armpits and my head bobbed out of the water. I gasped and coughed and cried.

'Shut *up*, stupid,' said Pearl, sitting up calmly. 'Call yourself a mermaid? You're not very good at swimming, are you? Better practise, eh?' She shoved me straight back under.

She didn't always have a go at drowning me. Big Mo was there a lot of the time – and even when she wasn't, Pearl could sometimes be perfectly ordinary, just splashing and telling silly jokes. In a way that made it worse, never quite knowing when she was going to turn.

But then *I* turned.

11

I tried to kill Pearl.

No I didn't.

I don't know. I don't know what's real any more. I just remember what they all said. Everybody asked me how it happened and I had to tell it again and again. They kept telling me to relax and take my time but I was so tense I was like a little iron kid. It would have taken a crowbar to unclench me.

I suppose I looked as guilty as hell. They all thought I'd pushed her deliberately. Maybe I did.

Pearl flew through the air, arms waving, legs kicking, mouth screaming, showing every single one of her pearly teeth. I thought she might land on her feet and come running straight up the stairs to get me. But she landed on her back with a thump, one of her legs sticking out sideways. I waited for her to start crying. She didn't make a sound.

I teetered at the top of the stairs, peering down at her. Big Mo and Little Pete and Esme and all the boys came running. They made a lot of noise on Pearl's behalf. Little Pete ran to call an ambulance while Big Mo crouched beside Pearl, holding her hand, talking to her. Pearl didn't reply. Her eyes were half open but she didn't seem to be looking at anyone.

'She's dead!' said one of the boys.

'No, she's not,' said Big Mo, but she didn't sound sure. 'What happened? Did Pearl slip?'

They all looked up the stairs at me.

'April pushed her!'

'Of course she didn't push her. Did you, April?'

I didn't say a word. I didn't dare. I was frightened Pearl was dead too – but that would mean she couldn't tell on me.

The ambulance came at last and Pearl was tied onto a stretcher and taken off in a big white van. Big Mo went with her. She didn't return all night. When she eventually came back after breakfast she was on her own.

'Pearl *is* dead!' said one of the boys.

They all stared at me in awe. My breakfast cornflakes hurtled upwards and made my mouth taste of sick.

'April's a murderer!'

They all hissed it, even Esme, though I don't think she knew what it meant.

'Stop that silly nonsense!' Big Mo snapped. She had dark circles under her eyes and her hair hung lankly. 'Pearl isn't dead, but she's a very poorly little girl. She's got a broken hip, a fractured leg, cracked ribs, sprained wrists. The poor little pet will be in hospital for weeks.'

I let out a squeak of relief.

'April, I need to talk to you,' said Big Mo, her voice very solemn. She took hold of me by the wrist – as if she couldn't quite bring herself to hold my hand – and dragged me off to her private sitting room.

We kids weren't usually allowed even a peep inside there. There were rumours that Big Mo and Little Pete had a television the size of a cinema screen and vast leather sofas and white fur rugs. The only television was smaller than our set in the children's room, the sofa was a sagging chintz similar to Big Mo's frocks and there were no rugs at all, just dull porridge-colour carpet. I stared at it all the time Big Mo was talking to me. She talked and talked and talked.

'Pearl told me everything, April,' she said.

I hung my head.

'Yes, well may you look guilty!' said Big Mo. 'You *did* push her, didn't you?'

I nodded forlornly.

'On purpose!' Big Mo persisted.

I had to agree.

'You could easily have killed her,' said Big Mo. 'The boys were right, you *could* have ended up a murderer. I should tell the police what really happened, April.'

I waited, my heart thudding.

'But we can't have a scandal here. I've fostered kiddies more than twenty years with never a moment's bother. I've looked after the naughtiest boys and no child's *ever* been hurt, not seriously – a few lumps and bumps, a black eye after a fist fight, but never anything like this. Pearl says you flew at her for no reason!'

I had my reasons. Pearl had been the murderer, four times over. She'd torn Bluebell, Daffodil, Violet and Rose into tiny shreds.

I'd tried to be so careful, never letting her see them. I'd played with them secretly inside my head whenever Pearl was around, making sure my lips didn't move, but I wasn't mad enough to hold the real paper girls anywhere near her. I kept changing their hiding place just in case. They lived in my shoebox and then they moved to my damp sponge bag and then they squashed up together inside the pages of *Where the Wild Things Are*.

They would have been safe – but Esme betrayed me. I'd let her play paper girls in that long-ago pre-Pearl time and she'd never forgotten it.

Esme and Pearl and I were in the children's room. Esme was flicking through one of Big Mo's magazines, licking her finger and turning each page so violently that they crackled.

'Quit that, Esme! You're getting on my nerves. What are you doing with it anyway? You can't even read.'

'I can read. I can read lots. I can read, can't I, April?' Esme protested.

'Yes, you can read great, Esme,' I said.

'Rubbish. She's useless at reading. She's totally thick,' said Pearl.

'I'm *not* thick, I'm thin, thin as a pin,' said Esme, sucking in her big tummy and preening in a parody of a fashion model.

Pearl mocked her but Esme didn't mind.

'Like these ladies,' said Esme, stabbing at the magazine photographs. Then she paused. 'Daffodil!' she said. 'Look, April, it's Daffodil!'

She was right. It was the same model,

though her hair was different and she was wearing beach clothes. It was very clever of Esme to spot her.

'Daffodil?' said Pearl. 'What are you two nut cases on about?'

'Daffodil one of April's special little paper ladies,' said Esme. 'She got one, two, three, *four* pretty paper ladies.'

'Shut *up*, Esme.'

But I was too late. Pearl knew now. It took her a while to find them. I started to think they might be safe inside my woolly winter sock, but Pearl was like a bloodhound.

I went to my room after tea one day and found my underwear drawer slightly open. I rummaged inside and found one sock – empty. And there was the other one, right at the bottom. Inside were the tiny snipped remains of my girls. I tipped them out onto the carpet, wondering if I could stick them together, maybe make up a missing part or two as I'd done before with Rose and her leg. No, Pearl had been too thorough with her snipping. She'd turned my girls into confetti.

I tried to imagine them in my head but

Pearl seemed able to snip inside me too. I couldn't make them up any more. Daffodil and Rose and Violet and Bluebell stayed little pieces of paper.

I started crying.

'What's up, April?' said Pearl, putting her head round my door. Her teeth gleamed. 'Oh, boo hoo, boo hoo, baby! Does diddums want her soppy dollies back, eh? Honestly, crying over bits of paper! You're even nuttier than old Esme. Look, snotty-nose, it's just *rubbish*!'

She picked up a handful of flower girls and tossed them in my face. Little shreds of yellow, red, purple and blue stuck in my hair and fluttered against my face.

I felt as if I'd been scattered too. I wanted Mummy, I wanted Daddy, but they weren't there any more. I had no one. I was no one.

Pearl rolled a tiny pink speck in her fingers, possibly part of Rose's new leg that I'd tried so hard to make a good match. Pearl laughed and flicked it away as if it was snot out of her nose. I suddenly couldn't stand it. I rushed at her. She saw I wasn't playing about. She ran for it but I caught up with her along the landing. I punched her hard in the chest and she staggered backwards – back and back, and then she wobbled and went right over, down the stairs.

'You pushed her on purpose, didn't you, April?' Big Mo repeated. 'For no reason whatsoever?'

I nodded, because I *did* push her, and it was for no reason Big Mo would ever understand.

I haven't ever told anyone, not even Marion.

12

Maybe Marion *would* understand. She's so strange. She'll make an endless fuss if I get a bit cheeky or forget to make my bed, acting like I'm the worst girl in the world, but she didn't flinch when she found out all my past history. She still took me on. She acts like she trusts me too, leaving her bag lying around, never locking her precious stuff away, even though she knows what I got up to at Sunnybank.

I got sent there because Big Mo felt I was a threat to the other kids. Sunnybank was a special Children's Home, a dumping ground for hard-to-place kids. They *were* hard too. Especially some of the big girls. Gina and Venetia and Rayanne had their own girls' gang. Gina was the eldest and the toughest. Everyone was frightened of Gina, even some of the Sunnybank staff. But I was OK because she took a shine to me.

I should go home now. I'm nearly at the station, Travelcard in my hand. With a bit of luck I could be back before Marion finishes her shift in the Oxfam bookshop. She'll just think I've been at school all day.

I was so mean to her this morning. OK, *she's* mean not letting me have a mobile but she was really trying hard with those earrings. I could say sorry and try them on and show her how pretty they look. She might have got me a birthday cake for tea. We were looking at them in Marks and Spencer only the other day. I could ring Cathy and Hannah and see if they want to come over to share my cake. Though I'll have to swear them to secrecy about my missing school.

I don't know what I'm going to tell them either. I could say I simply felt like bunking off but they'd be astonished. They think I'm such a good girl. They'd never in a million years believe all the stuff I got up to at Sunnybank.

It didn't look like a Children's Home. It was a big converted mock-Tudor house with a large garden. There was a round sun with rays carved into the front gate. I used to run my fingers up and down the slats as I swung on the gate. One time I stuck my finger in the hinge by mistake but Gina sucked it for me to stop it throbbing and then gave me a whole tube of Smarties.

I was Gina's special baby. She liked it when I acted younger than I was, like a really little kid, so I spoke with a lisp and sucked my thumb when I was around her. It was very hot that first summer at Sunnybank so Gina fixed me up my own little paddling pool in a big plastic basin. We'd sunbathe for hours, Gina's dark skin turning mahogany, but she was careful to slap lotion all over my skinny shoulders and arms and legs, watching over me just like Mummy.

She watched over me at nights too when she and Venetia and Rayanne smuggled me out after midnight. Not *every* night, only the times Billy or Lulu were in charge. They were both heavy sleepers and never stirred. Then Gina and her gang crept out – and a lot of the boys did too, though we never got involved with them. Gina got us girls organized into a highly efficient burgling team. I was Gina's key ingredient when it came to breaking and entering because I was so small.

Most people left their little bathroom windows open. Gina hoisted me halfway up every handy drainpipe and I clambered the rest of the way and then hooked my arm right through the window up to my shoulder, tucked my head right in tight, wriggled through up to my waist, tried to get my hands on the bathroom windowsill and then tumbled down, one leg after the other, to land in the washbasin.

I thought I was stuck for ever the first time, head in the stranger's bathroom, bottom and legs poking out into blank air behind me. I snivelled, teeth clamped in my bottom lip so I wouldn't make a sound, and then gave one last desperate wriggle and landed head first, my head catching such a clunk from the cold tap that I nearly knocked myself out.

I got a lot better at burgling but I always hated it. Sometimes I wet my knickers or worse during those night-thieving sessions, I was so scared of getting caught. I had to creep out of strange bathrooms in the pitch dark, find my way across the landing, holding my breath at each creak of the floorboards, listening for a lull in the snores behind the bedroom doors, looking over my shoulder constantly in case someone was creeping after me, ready to catch me and hand me over to the police.

I had to scamper down the stairs and then find out the way to open the back door for Gina – and Rayanne and Venetia too if they were all along for the laugh. They really *did* seem to find it fun. I hated every second even when everything went like clockwork – and often it *didn't*. One time I couldn't work out all the bolts and locks on the back door and twiddled and tugged for ages while Gina whispered impatiently from the garden. And then I heard the thump of someone's feet on the floor above my head and then the clomp, clomp of slippers coming down the stairs. I gestured frantically at Gina through the kitchen window. She pointed towards the front door – but the steps were nearly down in the hall by now and they'd catch me. I shook my head at Gina and she suddenly bobbed out of sight.

I thought she'd abandoned me and started crying but then she bobbed back, her shoe in her hand. She smashed the window, stuck her arm through, grabbed me and pulled. By the time the man reached the broken window we were right over the garden fence. I had glass in my hair and my hands were bleeding after all the tugging but at least we'd escaped. This time. It was so hard knowing there was going to be a next time – and a next and a next.

It wasn't just the fear of being caught. It was the terror of knowing I was going straight to Hell for being a thief. Mummy had taught me it was wrong to steal so much as a dropped grape in Marks and Spencer's food hall. When she'd caught me chewing she'd told me off so sorrowfully I wouldn't go to bed that night in case I was sucked straight to Hell in my sleep. I was April the Awful Grape-Stealer and I'd have to be good for the rest of my life to make up.

But I had very nearly murdered Pearl and so I was shut up with all these bad girls – and now I was bad too.

I suppose I didn't have much choice. You certainly couldn't argue with Gina. You didn't tell on her either. Not that there was really anyone to tell. The staff at the Children's Home kept changing. One woman arrived and immediately got into an argument with Venetia. Venetia slapped her and she slapped Venetia straight back so she had to leave an hour after she'd arrived, which was a quick turnover even for our Children's Home.

Billy had been there the longest but he was frightened of Gina and her gang. He was frightened of almost everyone. Even me. I learnt to look at him really hard, widening my eyes so that they nearly popped. It seriously unnerved him. He'd read my notes. Perhaps he thought I was selecting him as my next victim.

Lulu was kind in a soppy sort of way but she never really listened. She nodded and looked in your direction but she was only ever thinking about her boyfriend Bob, a big lollopy guy who came and watched television with her when she was working nights. They wore matching T-shirts. Lulu's said I LOVE BOB and Bob's said I LOVE LULU. Even when he wasn't around Lulu was still tuned into him, as if she were wearing invisible headphones.

So I kept quiet. I kept quiet at my new school too. I was tired of trying to make new friends so I kept to myself and hid in the toilets at playtime. I didn't say a word during lessons. It was more peaceful if everyone thought you were too thick to know any of the answers. I *felt* thick anyway, my brain in a fog, because I never had enough sleep. It was easy for Gina and Venetia and Rayanne because they went to secondary school by themselves so they could all bunk off but I was driven down to the primary school in the

Children's Home mini-bus. It had a big sun painted on both sides and the words SUNNY-BANK CHILDREN'S HOME but someone had spraypainted the S into an F and added FOR TOTAL NUTTERS. I felt as if I'd been spray-painted with the same scarlet paint.

I was sent once a week to a strange lady with a lot of toys in her office. I thought she was a special teacher and I was having extra-easy lessons but now I see she was probably some kind of psychiatrist. They needed to find out if I was really bad – or mad, a nutter just as my schoolmates suspected.

I couldn't decide which was worse. I knew I was bad. I was still haunted by Pearl and every time she came near me in my dreams. I'd give her another push. Now I was a thief too, up all hours with Gina night after night. The neigh-bourhood was fuming at all the break-ins. The police had visited the Children's Home making general inquiries. I nearly wet myself when I saw the men in uniform but Gina stayed calm, answering every question with off-hand grunts and shrugs. Venetia and Rayanne were equally nonchalant.

The boys all tried to be too smart, getting aggressive and alleging harassment. Gina grinned slyly, knowing they were the prime suspects.

Nobody thought about me. I wasn't even interviewed.

I didn't breathe a word about any of this during my therapy sessions. I played obediently with the weird dolls in the lady's office, handling them gingerly because they all had very rude-looking realistic bottoms. I rearranged the dolls' house, and put the mummy doll in the bath. I shut the daddy doll in the wardrobe. I twiddled the baby doll in my fingers. I couldn't find a toy dustbin.

I drew a dustbin with the lady's felt-tip pens but she started watching me and I got worried. I turned the dustbin into a big vase and drew flowers all different colours. Red and yellow and blue and purple. Then I cried but the lady didn't know why.

Gina saw I'd been crying when I got back to the Children's Home. I told her about Daffodil, Rose, Violet and Bluebell and how I still missed them. She thought I was daft carrying on about paper dolls that weren't worth a penny. I just hung my head, snivelling.

'Cheer *up*, April,' she said.

I tried but without much success.

'*I'll* cheer you up. You wait and see,' said Gina. She went round the shops on Saturday without me. She came back with a clutch of Barbie dolls and thrust them into my hands.

'There you are! *Real* dolls,' Gina said triumphantly. 'Much better than scrappy old paper dolls, eh?'

I fingered their pointy fingers and pointy breasts and pointy feet. I still secretly mourned my flower girls but the Barbie dolls were wonderfully glamorous. I couldn't play with them openly because Billy or Lulu would have wondered where on earth I'd got them from, but I had fantastic secret games with them in the wardrobe, the door just a little open to let in a chink of light. I pretended it was our house and Barbie-Ann and Barbie-Beth and Barbie-Chris and Barbie-Denise and I lived there together and styled each other's hair and swopped clothes and shared secrets.

Gina crawled into the wardrobe with me sometimes and played too. It was a bit of a squash because Gina was so big. She was impatient too, tugging the tiny outfits too hard and tearing seams but I couldn't very well shut her out.

One time one of the other girls got in; not Venetia or Rayanne, a sad, older girl called Claire with long straggly hair who wasn't friends with anyone. No one seemed to bother to speak to her. She can't have been that old because she went to the Juniors too though she looked like a teenager. She acted it too, hanging round the big boys and letting them do whatever they wanted.

Claire tried to make friends with me but Gina objected fiercely so that wasn't possible. She still crept into my room every now and then and once caught me playing with the Barbie dolls. She gazed at me beseechingly but I didn't dare invite her to join in my game in case Gina caught us.

The next day the Barbie dolls went missing. They weren't in their shoe-box bed at the back of the wardrobe. They hadn't crawled into the rubbery hidey-holes of my trainers or Wellington boots though I tipped them up to check. They hadn't hiked across the carpet on their tippy-toes to sneak a peak in my knicker drawer or play tents in my T-shirts. They weren't peeping out of my dressing-gown pocket or doubled up in my pencil case. They weren't anywhere at all, though I searched and searched and searched.

I knew Gina was going to go mad. She didn't go mad at me. She went mad at Claire, deciding she was to blame, even though I hadn't breathed a word that she'd seen the Barbies. She swore she didn't know what Gina was on about, keeping to her story even when Gina seized a hank of her stringy hair and pulled hard. I believed her and begged Gina to stop, but no one could stop Gina once she'd started. She slammed the poor girl against the wall and started searching through her bedroom, tearing it apart, ripping half her stuff. I started howling and Gina misunderstood.

'Don't you fret so, April. I'll get your Barbies back for you,' she said.

She flapped the duvet in the air, tossed the pillows around and then seized the mattress. Claire squealed and Gina jerked it upwards triumphantly. There were the Barbies entombed underneath, each wrapped in a white paper tissue like a shroud.

'I *knew* you had them, you dirty little thief,' spat Gina. 'Well, you'll be sorry now.'

Claire ended up very, very sorry, though I begged Gina to stop.

Gina was a thief too, of course. She'd probably stolen the Barbie dolls herself. But that was different. She'd stolen them for me. That sort of stealing didn't seem so bad when I was Sunnybank. It was the way you got things, the way you got your own back.

It makes me feel bad now. I don't want to think about it. So why am I getting on the wrong train at the station? Why am I going back to Sunnybank? Gina won't be there now. She'll be twenty-one, twenty-two. I can't imagine her grown-up. I wonder what she's doing now? Maybe she's locked up.

13

It's taken me a while to find it. I was starting to think I'd maybe made it all up. But here it is. Here's the gate with the sun's rays. I run my finger up and down them as I stare in at the white house with the yellow door. I don't feel anything. It's as if I'm acting in a film. This is just a wooden gate. Sunnybank is simply a big house. Maybe it's not even a Children's Home now.

Who am I kidding? There are toys littering the stubbly grass and bikes and skateboards are all over the porch. A battered mini-bus is parked in the driveway. I wonder if Billy still drives it?

I don't want to see him, or Lulu, even if they're still around. The only one I'd love to see is Gina.

I cried and cried when I had to leave Sunnybank. We got caught, Gina and me. Lulu and Billy were waiting up for us when we crept back into the house at dawn after a night's burgling. It was Claire. She told them. There was no way we could lie our way out of it. Gina had a stack of CDs tucked down her jacket and three hundred pounds and a handkerchief full of gold jewellery in her pockets.

So I got sent away to a special school. I don't know why they didn't send Gina away. Maybe she was too old or they felt she was too set in her ways. This new school was supposed to be giving me a new chance.

I didn't want to go but no one listened to me. That's the scariest thing of all about being in care. You don't get to choose. You just get shoved here, sent away there.

I felt I was being chucked out of Sunnybank because they'd got sick of me. I wasn't supposed to have anything to do with Gina that last week. There certainly weren't any more midnight jaunts. There was a new padlock and an alarm system put on the front door, the back door, even the windows. Lulu had a new regime too, getting up in the small hours to check we were all safely in our beds.

I waited until she'd padded round everyone. Then I crept out and went in search of Gina. I climbed into her bed and she gave me a big cuddle and called me her baby. I cried and I think Gina cried a bit too, because her cheek was wet when she gave me a kiss. We stayed cuddled up tight, me on Gina's lap, until morning.

I never saw her again. She did write to me once at the school but she wasn't really much of a letter writer so she just drew me a picture and signed her name very elaborately, swirls all down the page and then added lots of kisses.

I wrote to her every week for the first year

even though I gave up hoping for further replies.

Maybe I could write just one more time. The Sunnybank staff might have Gina's address. I open the sun gate and walk up the path. I stare at the door and then give the knocker two quick raps.

A blonde woman in dungarees answers, a teatowel tied round her waist. Her hair is divided into bunches with little bows. Lulu often had silly stick-out plaits. People who work with children often want to dress like them too.

'Lulu doesn't still work here, does she?' I ask.

She shakes her head so that her bunches waggle.

'I think there *was* a Lulu way back, but I never knew her.'

'What about Billy?'

The bunches waggle again.

'Did you want to get in touch with them then?'

'Well, not really. It was more this girl, Gina—'

'Oh, *Gina!*' she says.

'Do you know her?'

'Everyone knows Gina,' she says, smiling.

'But she can't still live here?'

'No, but she comes to visit us lots, and she's part of our lecture programme too.'

'Gina gives *lectures*?'

'She goes round all the Children's Homes in the South East area and talks to the kids. She's wonderful with them. They can really relate to her because she's been through the system herself. What about you?' She looks at my neat school uniform doubtfully. 'Did you ever live here?'

'Just for a bit. I was friends with Gina. But I think it was maybe a different Gina.'

'There's only one Gina! She lives near here, on the Kempton Estate. See those multi-storey flats? She lives on the top floor of the south block, number 144. Why don't you go and look her up? I'm sure she'd love to see you.'

I walk over to the flats though I'm sure it's pointless. She can't possibly be my Gina. This Gina gives lectures. The only subject my Gina could lecture on is breaking and entering.

This maybe isn't a good idea anyway. I don't know what this Kempton Estate is like. I've had enough of scary encounters. I keep looking round warily and when some little kid clatters up behind me on his skateboard I jump violently. The kid jeers at me and then whizzes on his way.

I try to stop being such a baby. The estate doesn't look too bad. I think some of it has gone private, because there are fancy curtains and potted plants in the windows and the front doors along the balconies are brightly painted in rainbow colours. I'm not so sure about the burnt-out bin area and the rude words all over the walls. I press the button for the lift, waiting an age, and then step in cautiously, avoiding a puddle.

I press for the top floor, but the lift stops halfway up and two guys with shaved heads and studs barge in. I swallow and take one step back. Thank goodness they act like I'm not even there. I look slyly at all their piercings, wondering what Marion would say if I came home looking like that. One of them sees I'm staring and sticks his studded tongue out at me. I laugh shakily and rush out of the lift on the fourteenth floor.

I feel as if I've stepped out onto the top of the world. I can see for miles and miles – but I have to grab the railing tight, feeling like I might be sucked straight over. I back along the balcony and find the front door of 144. I tap the knocker once, so softly maybe she won't hear. It won't be *my* Gina anyway.

A young woman comes to the door, barefoot, in jeans and a big blue shirt. A beautiful mop-haired toddler clings to her hip. She stares at us, her head on one side.

She's not Gina.

'I'm sorry,' I stammer. 'I was looking for . . .'

Is it Gina? She's big, she's broad, she's black, but she's so *different*. This Gina's adult and arty and attractive, with lovely long hair elaborately plaited and beaded. She's got a diamond nose stud and crescent moon silver earrings and bangles jingling up and down her plump arms. She doesn't look fierce, she's got a friendly smile on her face. It suddenly stretches wide.

'April!' she cries. 'My little April!'

She hugs me tight, her baby squashed between us. I breathe in her familiar warm, powdery, musky smell.

'It *is* you, Gina!' I say, and I burst into floods of tears.

'Yep, it's definitely you, April,' says Gina, laughing. 'You were always such a crybaby – but you were *my* baby, right? Hey, what do you think of my real baby, eh?' She holds her toddler up proudly, giving it a quick kiss and tickle. It snuggles sideways, chuckling.

'She's lovely.'

'*He!* He's my baby Benjamin. Don't worry, everyone thinks he's a girl because he's so gorgeous and I suppose it's the curls too. Everyone keeps on at me to take him to the barber's but it would be a crime to cut off all his curlylocks, wouldn't it, my little babe?'

Benjamin laughs and shakes his head so that his curls bob.

'Yes, you've got *lovely* curls,' I say, sniffing.

'You need a tissue, as always! Come on in, April. This is just so great! I can't believe it. How old are you now then? Eleven, twelve?'

'I'm fourteen. Today, actually.'

'Wow! Happy birthday, babe!'

She steers me inside with her free arm. The hall is swimming pool turquoise with dolphins diving up and down the walls. The living room is purple, with red curtains and big red velvet cushions and a giant black and white panda perched in his own red rocking chair. I follow Gina to her kitchen. It's canary yellow, so bright you need sunglasses. Gina hands me a hunk of kitchen roll, pops Benjamin into his highchair with a rusk and then puts the kettle on.

'I love your flat,' I say shyly, blowing my nose.

'Yeah, great, isn't it? I got some of the older kids from Sunnybank to help me paint it,' she says, setting out orange flowery mugs. 'Have you just been back there?'

'I was trying to find you.'

'Oh April, you're going to make *me* cry,' says Gina, giving me another hug. Then she laughs. 'Bet you were surprised to hear I'm Ms Goody-Goody-Gina nowadays? Remember all that stuff we used to get up to? You were a right little cat burglar when you were tiny! You'd shin up a drainpipe and wriggle through a window quick as a wink.'

'Did you find another little kid to help after I left?'

'No. They were all rubbish compared to you. And I kind of lost heart. I missed you, babe.'

'You didn't write.'

'Yes I did!'

'You sent a picture.'

'Well, I've never been into writing much – and you could never get near the computer at Sunnybank with all them boys. Anyway, I didn't really want to write. I wasn't very proud of myself. I was an idiot, I got into all sorts of stupid stuff, then I had a baby which was one big mistake.'

'Benjamin?'

'No, this was another kid. I was still just a kid myself.'

The kettle is starting to boil. I feel as if my own thoughts are bubbling.

'So what happened to it?' I say. 'Did you – did you give it away?'

A tear spills down Gina's cheek. 'She got taken away. I wasn't a good mother.'

'But you're wonderful with Benjamin!'

'I wasn't with my Amy. Oh, I loved her, I loved her to bits, but I was out of my head most of the time, using all sorts of stuff, not knowing whether I was coming or going. They'd given me this flat, tried to set me up, but I couldn't look after myself, let alone a baby. She was sick a lot. I got sick too. I was still thieving a lot of the time. I got caught and they sent me to this rehab place – and took Amy into care.'

'Oh, Gina.' I put my arm round her.

'No, don't feel sorry for me. It was my own fault. I was a mess. I screwed everything up.'

'But how could they take her away if you loved her? She was *yours*. Couldn't she have stayed with you?'

'Not at this place. Maybe I should have tried harder to keep her. I just felt she'd have a rotten life with me. I didn't think she'd want someone like me for her mum. I didn't want her passed round like a parcel, dumped in different Children's Homes like I was. So

I let her be adopted. She's got a lovely new family now.' Gina smiles, though tears are still sliding down her cheeks. 'Don't look at me like that, April. I thought it was for the best. She's happy now, I know she is. And I'm happy too. I went a bit crackers after I gave her up. I was in this special unit for a bit but I got my head together eventually, gave up all my bad habits – and now look at me!

'I've still got to sit some exams. It takes me ages, you know what I'm like at writing, but I'm getting there. I'm going to be a social worker. I'm not going to be an old softie. I'm going to give those kids hell if they don't toe the line – but at least I'll know what it's like for them. They won't be able to kid me. I've been there, done that, messed up in every kind of way. I do this talk, right, telling the kids all about it. Some of the hard nuts don't want to know but some of the younger ones feel a bit of respect for me.'

'I feel respect for you, Gina,' I mumble, blushing because it sounds a bit daft.

'So I should hope!' says Gina. She makes us a both a mug of tea and gives Benjamin a bottle of milk. Then she grins at me. 'OK, April, what do birthday girls get?'

I blink at her.

'Cake!' Gina opens a cupboard and takes out a huge tin. She opens it with a flourish. I see half a pink iced sponge studded with Smarties with 'Happy Birthday' in swirly writing. 'I knew you'd come today!'

I gape at her. Gina laughs.

'I'm teasing, nutcase. I made it for one of the kids along the balcony. I run this club, see, a play scheme thing. Benjamin loves it because everyone wants to play with *him*. Whenever it's anyone's birthday I make a cake.'

I think of Marion at home, maybe with a Marks and Spencer's birthday cake set set on her special crystal plate. She'll be wondering why I'm late home from school. She'll be starting to get worried.

If I had a mobile I could ring her. It's her own fault.

That's rubbish. I'm rubbish.

I can't stop thinking about her all the time I'm chatting to Gina and eating birthday cake and feeding Benjamin little slithers of icing.

I could ask Gina if I could use her phone. I want to. But I can't. Marion will want to know where I am. If she finds out I've bunked off school she'll go really mad.

I could tell her I'm at Cathy's or Hannah's. But then she'll want to come round to collect me. It's too complicated.

I won't phone her but I'll go home straight away and I'll tell her how sorry I am and I'll make it up to her somehow.

'I'd better get going, Gina. My foster mum will be wondering where I've got to.'

'You're a good girl, April,' says Gina.

I'm bad, I'm bad, I'm bad.

Gina gives me a huge hug when we say goodbye. I cling to her, wishing I was as little as Benjamin so she could carry me around all day.

'You'll keep in touch now, babe,' says Gina. 'Write to me? I'll write back properly this time, I promise.'

I go down in the smelly little lift, trying not to cry. When I get out into the courtyard and look up I see Gina standing way up on the balcony. She's clutching Benjamin tightly with both hands so she can't wave but she bobs her head at me and he does too. They look like two dark flowers blowing in the wind.

Gina's a wonderful mum.

I wonder if *my* mum ever got a second chance.

14

I've got to go home.

I'm on the tube, on my way to Waterloo. I'll make up some story for Marion. I've made up stories for me enough times.

This story doesn't have a happy ending. I haven't found her.

No that's silly. I've found two great friends, a new one and an old one. I've found my very first foster mother and the grave of my adoptive mother. I've found so many people today – but I still feel lost. Lonelier than ever. There's only one person I want.

How can I ever find her? She could be anywhere at all. Like looking for a needle in a haystack. Tealeaf in a dustbin.

The Dustbin Baby.

There's one more place.

I have a Travelcard. I can journey on from Waterloo.

Or I can go home to Marion.

I'm no good at making decisions. When I first went to live with Marion I couldn't even choose what I wanted for tea. You didn't get a choice at Fairleigh. You just got your baked beans or your scrambled eggs – splat – on your plastic platter. You got iced buns afterwards on a Friday, for a treat, pink ones with jam or white ones with currants or yellow ones with a cherry on top but I was such a slow eater they'd mostly all gone by the time I'd cleared my platter. You had to finish all your main course. It was one of the rules. Sometimes I got a big girl called Julie to eat mine for me, surreptitiously shovelling forkfuls from my plate as well as hers, but then she got friendly with an anorexic girl who paid her twenty pence a plate so Julie concentrated on helping her out instead.

I don't need to go on a nostalgic trip back to Fairleigh. I lived there for five years, longer than I've ever lived anywhere else. I didn't even go away any place in the holidays, apart from one sad summer camp for children with special needs, where I mostly helped the helpers.

Marion and I are going on holiday this summer. Italy. Five days doing all the culture and history and art stuff, but then five days by the sea for me.

'It's only fair. It's your holiday as much as mine,' she said.

She *is* fair, even though she's so fussy. It's getting so late. What am I going to do if she's phoned Cathy or Hannah and they tell her I wasn't at school? I wish I was at Cathy's or Hannah's now. I mostly feel so *ordinary* with them. We have a laugh together and a moan about the teachers and a sigh about boys and a wail about our hair/spots/figures. We might talk about what we want to happen in our lives but we never talk about who we are or where we come from.

They're the friends I've always longed for. I had friends at Fairleigh but they were odd friends, sad girls, bad girls, mad girls – like me. That's why we got sent there. It's a school for vulnerable girls: girls constantly in trouble; girls with special needs; girls with learning difficulties; girls in distress. We were all lumped together and dressed alike in our blue-and-white checked dresses and blue blazers. We were all given identical teddy bears with blue knitted jerseys to take to bed at night.

During the day we were put into very small classes so we could have individual attention. I didn't *want* attention. I wanted to hide inside myself and keep out of trouble. There were quite a few Down's girls at the school like Esme back at Big Mo's. I made friends with a very kind Down's girl in my year, called Poppy. She loved sweets. She bought a lollipop every day from the school tuckshop.

'I'm Lollipoppy,' she'd chortle, over and

over, sounding so funny and daft she got me giggling too.

I wanted to sit beside Poppy in classes and do colouring with her big wax crayons. She had special alphabet pictures. I thought how peaceful it would be to colour in 'A is for Apple, B is for Baby, C is for Cat', but I had to do sums and science and stories. I didn't know how to add up or experiment or invent so I was useless at first. I thought it was because I was simply thick. I didn't realize it was because I'd been in and out of so many schools I'd missed out on learning all the really basic stuff.

They did their best to remedy this at Fairleigh. After a term or two I felt as if someone had stuck a pair of strong spectacles on my nose. I could see straight at last. It wasn't comfortable. I preferred seeing inside my own head. There wasn't time to daydream now. I had to think, to work things out, to come up with answers.

Maths and Science and Technology stayed a struggle but I liked English and I *loved* History. Miss Bean made it fun. She was older than the other teachers and she looked a sight in terrible hand-knitted jumpers in pastel colours, baby blue and pale pink and insipid lilac. We all called her the Beanie Baby – but not to her face.

No one dared be naughty in Miss Bean's class. She was much stricter than the other teachers. She nagged me something rotten. '*Try*, April!', 'Come along, *think*!', 'No this isn't good enough, you can do better than that'. But sometimes she could make things magic. Especially History.

We did the Romans and she let us take the sheets off our beds to wrap round us like togas. We had a Roman feast with wine (Ribena) and all sorts of sweetmeats (Miss Bean provided homemade fudge and toffee and coconut ice, plus an extra lollipop to keep Poppy happy). We made our own special model of the Colosseum (she showed us photos of it from her summer holiday in Rome) with tiny cardboard Romans and wild animals and Christian martyrs. I felt a pang seeing these little cardboard figures, remembering poor Bluebell, Rose, Daffodil and

Violet, but I quickly entered into the spirit of the thing. I fashioned some especially ferocious wild animals and then cut out a champion gladiator with a gilt-sprayed toothpick sword in his clenched fist.

'Well *done*, April!' cried Miss Bean.

I really came into my own when we did the Victorians. I settled down happily to making an elaborate Victorian villa out of a big cardboard box and a stack of cornflake packets, copying the details from the pictures in the Victorian history books in the library – but some of the slower girls got everything mixed up and wanted another toga party with wine.

'No, no, that was the Romans. They lived hundreds and hundreds of years before the Victorians,' said Miss Bean.

They still couldn't get it. It was all History to them. The Victorians were every bit as ancient as the Romans.

'I'll tell you what we'll do,' said Miss Bean. 'We'll all do our family trees and then you'll see that your very own great-great-great grandmothers were Victorians.'

I kept very still. I didn't join in the silly

jokes about family trees and Great-Auntie Oak and Grandpa Maple. I didn't even pick up my pen. I sat with my hands clasped in my lap, my nails digging into my palms.

Miss Bean bobbed around the class in her baby-blue jumper, giving advice here and there. She printed 'Mummy' and 'Daddy' in pencil on Poppy's piece of paper and Poppy traced over the top with red wax crayon, her tongue sticking right out with the effort of keeping to the lines.

Miss Bean looked over in my direction. 'Come on, April. Get cracking.'

I sat tight.

She came over to me, frowning. 'April! What's the matter with you this morning? Get started!'

'I don't want to.'

'What did you say?'

'I said I don't want to,' I repeated very loudly.

The whole class put down their pens and watched, mouths open.

'I don't care what you want. You'll do as you're told in my classroom,' said Miss Bean.

She tapped my blank page. 'Get started this instant, April.'

'You can't make me, you stupid old fat Beanie Baby!' I shouted.

Everyone sat stunned. Even I wasn't quite sure I'd really said it.

'I don't allow that sort of rudeness in my classroom,' said Miss Bean. 'Go outside and stand in the corridor.'

I stumbled down the rows of desks to the door. I wondered whether to make a run for it once I was outside. But there were no really foolproof hiding places in the school. I'd tried the toilets and the games cupboard and the boiler room but I'd always been discovered. There was outside – but I had scarcely been out of the grounds since I'd arrived and the whole idea of outside seemed as alien as Mars. So I stood miserably in the corridor, waiting for the end of the lesson.

Hours and hours and hours seemed to go by.

My own words echoed in my head. 'You can't make me.' But this was Miss Bean and she probably had many unpleasant ways of making me do anything she wanted. I imagined increasingly outlandish tortures, most of them incorporating the sharp and very whippy cane on show in the Victorian project display.

The girls came out at long last, staring at me in awe. Then Miss Bean beckoned to me from the doorway.

'Come into the classroom, April.'

Once we were inside she shut the door.

'I don't want you to speak to me in that tone of voice ever again,' she said gravely. 'Please apologize for your rudeness.'

'I'm sorry, Miss Bean,' I mumbled.

She nodded. Then she said something amazing. 'Now it's *my* turn to apologize to you. I feel I made a mistake asking you to compile your family tree. There may be all sorts of reasons why this is not a good idea. I should have thought first before I suggested it. I'm sorry, April. I hope you will accept my apology.'

'Yes, Miss Bean! I didn't mean to call you names. Well, I did, but it was just because I felt so weird when I couldn't fill anything in. I haven't *got* any family.'

My voice started to wobble. Miss Bean's face went blurry as I started to cry. Once I started I couldn't stop. I howled and howled. Miss Bean patted me on the shoulder, murmuring, 'There, there.' She offered me a little folded wad of tissue and I blotted my face as best I could.

'Better now?' she said softly. 'You run along to your next lesson then, dear.'

I ran. I was so tear-stained that everyone was sympathetic, convinced Miss Bean had been furious. I didn't tell anyone what had really happened. It seemed private between us.

15

Marion

Miss Bean and I were friends after that. Not
friends friends. She was still very much Miss
Ultra-Strict-Schoolteacher but she would give
me the glimmer of a smile every so often in
class and if I hung back she'd chat to me.
Sometimes she'd pick out a book for me or give
me a postcard of a painting. Then one
Saturday while we were still studying the
Victorians she turned up at the school and

told me she was taking me out for the day.

'If you'd like that, April,' she said.

I wasn't too sure that first time. I was still a little scared of her and I thought it would probably be boring to be stuck with her all day. I liked the way she taught History but I didn't fancy a History lesson all day long.

It wasn't like that at all. She did take me to the Victoria and Albert Museum but she made it great fun, and she took me to the shop afterwards and bought me a tiny bear dressed up as Queen Victoria. We went to the cafe too which seemed very grand and grown up. She said I could choose whatever I wanted.

'*Whatever?*' I said, staring at the wonderful cakes and puddings.

I couldn't choose between the chocolate gâteau or strawberries and cream, but she let me have both, though she insisted I have a little salad first. Miss Bean had wine with her meal which surprised me. I wondered if she might start acting drunk like Daddy, but she sipped her way through two glasses with no obvious effect.

I thought we'd catch the train straight back

to school now we'd marched all round the museum but Miss Bean suggested a little look round the shops first. She took me to Harrods. I felt as if I'd entered a fairy-tale palace. I tip-toed round, awestruck. The food hall was particularly astonishing, especially the chocolates. Miss Bean let me choose one of the white cream chocolates. She laughed at the expression on my face when I bit into it.

'Good?'

'Wondrous!'

'Have just one more. And I will too. Blow my boring old diet!'

She patted her large tummy. She was wearing her favourite pink jumper which made her look like a giant marshmallow but I didn't care. I *liked* her.

She took me out a lot after that. She usually drove us out into the country and we went for long walks. She told me about the trees and the birds and the wild flowers. I didn't always listen. I liked to think my own thoughts and wonder where we might go for afternoon tea. I pretended we were related and this was a normal weekend visit. She didn't seem the granny type and clearly she couldn't be my *mother*, so I turned her into my eccentric great-aunt.

The girls at Fairleigh teased me when they found out about the Saturday outings. Someone said Miss Bean might be after me and I'd better watch out. I hissed in Gina's most menacing tones that they'd better shut up or I'd sort them out. They left me alone after that.

Miss Bean was getting near retiring age. I suppose I should have realized. It came as a shock the summer term I was in Year Seven when she said she'd be leaving in July. I didn't know what to say. I screwed up my face to stop myself bursting into tears.

'Are you going to miss my History lessons that much, April?' she asked jokingly.

'I'm going to miss *you*,' I blurted out.

Miss Bean pulled her own face. 'Well . . . I could always come and visit you. We could still go out at weekends if – if you'd like to.'

'I would!'

'I would too. I enjoy our outings very much. But you must promise me you mustn't feel

171

obliged to trail round with me. I can never tell if you're just being polite.'

I still wasn't sure she'd really come calling for me. I cried the last day of term when Miss Bean said goodbye to everyone in Assembly and the head girl presented her with a clock and a suitcase and a set of history books. Surprisingly lots of the other girls cried too. I was pleased Miss Bean was popular even though she was so old-fashioned and strict. Poppy was in floods of tears. Miss Bean gave her a big bunch of lollipops as a goodbye present. She didn't give me anything, but she patted my shoulder as she passed and whispered, 'I'll come soon, April, I promise.'

She packed her new suitcase and went abroad on holiday but she sent me two postcards – and the first weekend she was back she arrived at Fairleigh early on Saturday morning. She had a new short haircut, a deep tan, and bright blue baggy trousers that really suited her though they made her bottom look even bigger.

'Come on, April,' she said.

'You look so different!'

'I *feel* different,' she said, flipping her fingers through her short hair.

She said I didn't have to call her Miss Bean now she'd stopped being my teacher. I could call her by her first name. Marion.

She chatted to the other teachers when she came to collect me, and she always made a fuss of Poppy, but she was really there to see me. She said she didn't miss teaching. She was busy learning Italian and playing the piano and running an Oxfam bookshop three days a week. She was also busy moving, from a flat in town to a bungalow in the suburbs. She took me to see it before she moved in.

'I need to know what you think of it, April,' she said.

I didn't quite see what she was getting at. She skirted around things for months. She talked about my future and what I wanted to do. I said I'd wondered about being a dress designer (snipping and sewing red, yellow, blue and violet outfits) but Marion suggested a History degree. She tried very gently to make me talk about my own history. I hated this. I knew I was a Dustbin Baby. I remembered as far back as Mummy and Daddy, though most of the details were sketchy, but I didn't want to think about it. It always gave me a shaky feeling, as if I was standing on the edge of a cliff.

I couldn't understand why Marion had started probing when she could see it upset me. We were usually scrupulous about each other's feelings. I never talked about diets or exercise or fat people (Marion had put on more weight since leaving school and had had to buy even baggier trousers) and she never talked about mothers.

'Do shut *up* about it, Marion,' I said eventually, as we walked round the formal gardens of Hampton Court.

I put my hand over my mouth once the words were out, scared that Marion would turn back into Miss Bean and punish me.

She seemed upset, not cross, though she automatically told me not to talk in that rude tone of voice.

'Say "be quiet" if you must, but never tell anyone to shut up.'

'Well, OK, please be quiet and quit going on and on about all my foster mothers,' I said, scuffing my sandals in the chalky gravel.

'I hope you're going to polish those the minute you get back to school,' said Marion. She paused. 'I take it you didn't like being fostered?'

'No!'

'And – and you don't want to be fostered again?'

I looked at her warily.

'What do you mean? *Is* someone going to foster me?' I started to panic.

'Not if you don't want it to happen.'

'Well, I don't. You mean stop boarding at Fairleigh?'

'That's maybe not such a bad idea. You're very bright, April, even though you've still got a lot of catching up to do. If you went to a proper secondary school you could take your GCSEs and A-levels and—'

'And read History at university, yeah, yeah, I know. Though I'm *not* bright, I'm rubbish at heaps of things.'

'And you don't seem exactly *happy* at school. You haven't got many friends, apart from Poppy.'

'I'm OK. I don't want heaps of friends. Anyway, I've got you. If I get fostered I wouldn't be able to see you at weekends, would I?'

'You could maybe see a lot more of me.'

'How?'

Marion laughed nervously.

'Maybe you're not so bright after all, April. I want to be your foster mother.'

I stared at her. She bravely met my eyes. 'You probably think it's a ridiculous idea. It *is*. I mean, I'm much too old and I'm single – though I've had a detailed chat with social services and they seem to think these aren't insurmountable problems. But of course you should really be with a proper family.'

'I don't want a proper family!'

I thought about it, my head whirling. I wasn't sure I wanted Marion either. She was good as my teacher, fine as my friend – but she wasn't a bit like a *mother*. I couldn't imagine living with her all the time.

I saw her bite her lip worriedly. I was being cruel keeping her waiting. So I took a deep breath.

'Thank you very much. It's very kind of you,' I said politely, as if she'd offered me a cup of tea rather than a permanent home. I struggled harder. 'It will be . . . wonderful.'

Marion smiled wryly.

'It won't be wonderful living with a grumpy old stick like me. I'll nag you about homework and I'll lecture you silly and I'll twitch terribly if you shorten your skirt or wear too much make-up. But I think we *could* get on well together. I'd love to give it a try. Of course I know I can't be like a real mother to you, April, but—'

'I don't want you to act like a real mother.' I still had one, even though I didn't have any idea who she was. And I'd had too many foster mothers to want another, even if that had to be Marion's official title.

Will I call you Mum or Auntie or what?'

'I think you should just carry on calling me Marion. Though if you're really bad we'd better go back to Miss Bean!'

It took a long time to get everything properly sorted out. Marion had to go on a special course. I had to see a new social worker,

Elaine. There were lots of meetings about me, nearly all behind my back.

'It's *my* life, so why can't I be there?' I asked Elaine.

'I know, it does seem stupid, April, but it's just the way we work,' she said, playing around with a little bunny on her desk.

'Why is it taking such ages? Marion wants to foster me and I want to be fostered by her so why can't we just get on with it?'

'I know, it's such a bore, but we've got to proceed carefully, prepare both of you, compile all the reports—'

I suddenly felt sick. Will Marion have to see all the stuff about me in my file?'

'I think she's seen it already,' she said gently.

'I thought that was *private*! You mean she knows about the times I went out thieving with Gina?'

'Yes.'

'And – she knows about *Pearl*?'

'Yes.'

'And she still wants to foster me?'

'She does.'

That silenced me. Elaine reached across her

desk and patted my hand. 'Marion understands, April. Don't worry. I don't think there'll be any problems about her fostering you. One of my other clients has recently been fostered by a single woman and that seems to be working well. I'm sure it will all work out beautifully for you and Marion.'

It has worked. But maybe not *beautifully*.

I left Fairleigh. Everyone sang a song for me the last day to wish me luck. Poppy sang an old Shirley Temple song, 'On the good ship Lollipop' – she just sang those five words all the way through until the music stopped. I laughed and then I cried and couldn't stop. I didn't really like Fairleigh but I'd lived there five years so it was like home. I didn't fit in but that was nothing new. I didn't fit in anywhere.

I wondered if I'd ever fit in with Marion. I had my own blue bedroom, with blue floral curtains and a matching duvet. She'd even bought me a new blue nightie and a blue quilted dressing-gown. I would have liked a brighter blue and I prefer wearing pyjamas and I don't ever bother with a dressing-gown but I pretended to be very grateful. I tried giving Marion a hug but we'd been teacher and pupil too long. We both found embracing embarrassing.

Marion hasn't ever tried to kiss me goodnight but she pats my shoulder and then tucks the duvet tight round my neck and under my chin. I always rear up out of it the moment she goes out the room. I hate anything round my head. If I burrow under the covers by accident in my sleep I always wake up in a panic.

Maybe I was stuck in that dustbin for hours and hours.

Of course I can't remember what it was like. It just seems as if I can. I'm nearly there. I'm off the train, on the tube. There's no stopping me now. I know where I'm going.

I have to find The Pizza Place in the High Street. If it's still there. Even if it is, it's mad to think there'll still be the same dustbins round the back. And even madder to think my mother will be there.

Marion is almost as good as a real mother. She's been so kind to me. It's cruel of me to keep her worrying at home, wondering where on earth I am.

She won't be *really* worried. She'll be anxious, she'll be concerned, like a teacher when someone goes missing from the playground. But I've seen mothers lose their children. I've seen that terrible chewed-up look on their faces, heard their high-pitched calling. I've seen Cathy and Hannah's mums the day the school coach got a double puncture and we were all hours late after a trip to the Science Museum. Marion looked perfectly calm and collected. She'd spent her time reassuring everyone that we were all OK, school coaches were forever breaking down and we'd all turn up safe and sound.

Safe and sound. These are the words that sum her up, though she'd circle them in an essay and say I was using tired language. She's so safe you can believe everything she says. and never feel she's going behind your back to get rid of you. She's so sound you know there's no nasty rotten bit of her ready to turn sour on you. She's there, safe and sound, if you want her.

I do want her.

I want my *mum* too.

16

The Pizza Place is still there, halfway down the High Street, by a little alleyway. I peer in the window, looking at all the people eating their pizzas. I can't see anyone on their own. No woman looking out the window, waiting for me.

I walked past, down the alleyway.

She's not here.

I don't know why I'm crying. Of course she isn't here.

I'm in the right place. There's the dustbin. Well, it's not one single silver dustbin the way I'd imagined. There are lots of wheely-bins, large, stinking and unattractive. I don't know if there was a real dustbin once or whether the journalists fudged things because Wheely-bin Waif has less impact. I stare at the wheely-bins, breathing shallowly. How could anyone stuff a newborn baby in those dank depths? I've imagined it over and over and yet I've never thought about the *smell*.

I must have reeked when that boy raked through the rubbish and found me. Yet he cradled me inside his shirt. That's what the newspaper said. Maybe it just made a good story.

It's *my* story and I don't know what's made up and what isn't. I've made some of it up myself to fill in the gaps. I feel as if I'm not real. Everyone makes up their own version of me.

I don't know which is the real me. I don't know who I am.

Why can't she be here for me? Doesn't she even remember me on my birthday? Doesn't she ever wonder what I've turned out like? I've thought about her every day of my life.

She doesn't care. She gave birth to me but she shoved me straight in that bin and hasn't given me a second thought since. What sort of a mum could throw her baby away? Maybe she isn't worth finding. It's obvious she doesn't want me to look for her. She left me without a note, without a stitch of clothing, not even a nappy.

I punch the nearest wheely-bin. It hurts a lot. My knuckle starts bleeding and I suck it. Someone's scrawled rude words all over the bin. I say them too. There are numbers as well. A line of eleven numbers. Someone's left their phone number. There's a message in the same handwriting: PLEASE CALL, BABY.

I read it again and again and again.

It's a message for me.

No, that's crazy. It's nothing to do with me. Some girl and boy use this alley as their secret meeting place and now they need to get in touch. 'Baby' is a common enough nickname. Grant called Hannah 'Baby'. She thought it wonderful (though Cathy and I privately agreed it was a bit demeaning, like he couldn't be bothered to remember her name).

But maybe 'Baby' really does mean me. She might not have read the newspaper articles to know my name. So that's all she can call me. Baby. Her Baby. That's her telephone number. All I have to do is call her . . .

I've got a pound in my pocket. I could do it now.

I must call Marion too. I will. When I've worked out what I'm going to do. I fish in my pocket and find Tanya's card. I write down the number from the bin, and the message too. It seems to have more meaning written in my own handwriting.

I walk out of the alleyway, my legs trembling. I walk past the people eating supper in the Pizza Place window, along to the phone box down the road.

I can just ring that number and talk to her at last.

If I want.

Of course I want.

I'm not so sure. I'm scared. What if she's not the way I imagine? What if she's really tough or scary or stupid? I won't be able to make her up any more if I know what she's really like. I won't be able to make excuses for her if I know the real reason why she dumped me in that dustbin.

I've got to call her. She's sitting there at home, waiting and hoping. Maybe she's trekked to the alley behind The Pizza Place for years just in case. Maybe she's been trying desperately hard to get in touch all this time. Longing for us to be reunited. Maybe she's missed me as much as I've missed her.

I want to call her so badly.

I'm so scared of speaking to her.

I don't have to say anything. I can just dial the number and listen. Hear her voice.

I go in the phone booth and fumble for my pound. I drop it because my hands are shaking so badly. The floor smells like someone used it as a toilet. I feel sick. What am I doing here? Why don't I go home? *Phone* home at least. Tell Marion I'm safe and I'm coming home soon.

What if I phone my real mother and she says she wants me back? What if we meet and hug and can't ever let each other go? What will I do about Marion?

I can't phone her.

I want to phone someone else first to ask them what to do.

Shall I phone Cathy or Hannah? They're my friends. They're always there for me. But if I start telling them I'll never stop – and they won't understand.

I dial Tanya's number instead. She answers on the very first ring.

'Hi! It's Tanya,' she says breathlessly.

'It's me, Tanya. April. I'm sorry, are you expecting someone else to ring? I'll phone you back if you like.'

'No, no, it's fine, truly. Well – hi, April.'

'Tanya, I don't know what to do. I've got this phone number. It could just be my mother's. Well, it probably isn't. But I'm scared to try it. Does that sound mad?'

'A bit!'

'Don't you ever get scared?'

'Nope! Well, maybe. But you've got to go for what you want.'

'I don't *know* what I want. I mean, if it is my mum and she's nice and she's pleased to find me then, of course, that's what I want. But what if she's not the way I want her to be? What if—'

'Oh, stop all this what-iffy rubbish. Phone her! Look, give her a bell and then get straight back to me to tell me how it went.'

'I won't have enough change. I'll have to ring you later.'

'You should get a mobile.'

'I know.'

'Mine's a really cool model. You can get all sorts of messages, take two calls at once, whatever.'

'Great.'

Tanya sighs. 'Only no one's actually sent me a message yet. Or called me.'

'Well – *I've* called you. And you've been very helpful.'

'So you'll phone the number?'

'Yes.'

'It'll be OK. Trust your Auntie Tanya.' She sounds cheerful again. 'I'll start one of them advice hotlines on my mobile, right? Go on, April. Give it a try. Go for it.'

So I say goodbye. Just forty pence left, the display tells me. Maybe I'll wait till I get home and ring from there? There's hardly going to be any time to say anything.

How long does it take to say, 'Hello, are you my mum?'

Why can't I just get *on* with it?

I dial the number. It rings once, twice, three times – and then somebody picks up the phone. 'Hello?'

Oh God. It's a man's voice. What am I going to do now? I swallow. No words come out.

'Hello?' he repeats.

I don't have to say anything. I can just put down the phone.

'Don't hang up,' he says quickly, as if he can read my mind. 'Who are you?'

'You – you don't know who I am.'

'You're not the baby? Well, of course you're not a baby now. Are you the little girl who was found in the dustbin?'

189

'I'm not a little girl. I'm fourteen.'

'Fourteen today,' he says. 'Happy birthday, April. You are still April, aren't you?'

'Yes. But how do you know?' I stop. 'Are you my *dad*?'

'No! Though it's weird, I've always thought about you like you were my little kid. I just can't believe I'm talking to you. I couldn't get you out of my mind. I tried to find you ages ago but they said you'd been adopted and I didn't want to bring up the past and muck things up for you. I didn't know what they'd told you. Still, you must know about the dustbin if you've got my number.'

'So are you the boy who found me? Frankie?' I look at the phone. 'Oh no, I'm running out of money!'

'OK. Dial the operator and reverse the charges to me.'

The pips go.

'Promise me you will, April? Straight away?'

'I promise,' I say, and then we're cut off.

I dial the operator, I tell her the number, and then we're talking again.

'Thank you so much! I've waited fourteen years to find you – I couldn't bear to lose touch now!' he says. 'Where are you? Can we meet?'

'I'm just up the road from that Pizza Place.'

'Then let's meet now! I'm only about twenty or thirty minutes' drive away. Is that OK? Can we have a pizza together?'

'Yes, that's fine.'

'Who's with you?'

'No one.'

'What? You're there all by yourself!' He sounds like he really is my dad.

'I'm fine.'

'Oh come on! What about your family? Do they know where you are?'

'Well, there's my foster mum, and . . . well, no, she doesn't actually know I'm here.'

'Won't she be worried?'

I swallow. 'Yes.'

'April? Don't cry.'

'I haven't phoned her. I kept on meaning to but I didn't dare and now . . .'

'Here's what we'll do. You phone her now. Tell her where you are. Tell her I'm going to be with you very shortly. Then either I'll drive you home, or if she's uncomfortable about that I'll stay with you at The Pizza Place until she can come for you herself. April? Have you got that?'

'I think so.'

'You will phone her right away – reverse the charges again, OK?'

'Yes.'

'And then you'll go straight to The Pizza Place and order a meal – I'll pay for it when I get there, obviously.'

'It's . . . it's very kind of you.'

'I've dreamt of this moment! Ever since I tucked you inside my shirt—'

'You really did that, like it said in the newspapers?'

'Of course I did. You didn't have any clothes. You were freezing cold. I had to keep you warm.'

'So my mother didn't even wrap a shawl or sweater round me?'

'Well, I wouldn't imagine she was really prepared for you.'

'There was no sign of her?'

'No. I kept an eye on the dustbins for ages but she didn't show up. And I look on April 1st most years and I leave a message. My wife thinks I'm a bit cracked.'

'You're married?'

'And I've got two little boys and both times when they were born I held them in my arms – and thought about you. I so badly wanted to see you to make sure you were all right. April, are you all right? You said you've got a foster mum now? You get on with her?'

'Yes. Though she'll be so mad at me now.'

'Phone her! And I'll give you my mobile number so she can phone me. She might not like the idea of my meeting up with you.'

'But you're the one who saved my life!'

'That sounds dramatic. Someone else would have come along sooner or later. But I'm so glad it was me. OK, I'll be with you as soon as I possibly can. I've got dark hair, tallish, blue denim jacket . . .'

'I'm little, long fair hair—'

'That's exactly the way I've always pictured you! Oh, I can't wait to see you.'

I'm shaking as I put the phone down. He really means it. He really cares about me, even though we're not related.

Marion really cares about me even though we're not related. I was kidding myself before. I don't always *want* her to care but she does. The slightest little thing can send her into a state. She got terribly fussed when I had my ears pierced in case the equipment hadn't been sterilized properly. She drove me to the hospital one time when I had a bad migraine just to check it wasn't meningitis. She *was* worried that time the school coach broke down. She pretended she was fine and acted all organized and efficient, but she'd picked at the ribbing on her pale pink jumper so violently that it started to unravel and she never wore it again.

She *would* hug me if I let her. She's tried several times. I'm the one who always backs away. It's because I don't want her to get too close. I don't want her to be a real mum. Because she's *not* my mum.

I've hung on so long hoping to find my real mum. I don't think I'm ever going to find her now. *She's* the one who hasn't been the *real* mum.

I dial the operator. I tell her Marion's number. She asks Marion if she'll accept the call. And then we're talking. Well, I can't talk. properly. I'm crying too much.

'Oh Marion, I'm sorry, I'm so sorry . . .'

'Are you all *right*, April?' Marion sounds desperate.

'Yes, I'm OK. In fact the most amazing things have happened. But I should have phoned you, I know. Have you been really really worried?'

'Of course I have! I've even been in touch with the police.'

'Oh no! Are they after me?'

'Looking out for you, you silly girl. To bring you home safe and sound. Where have you been? I've rung Cathy and Hannah, and everyone I could think of . . . I've spoken to Elaine . . . I told her all about the argument this morning.'

'I'm sorry, Marion. I was so mean and un-grateful. They're lovely earrings.'

'Do you know something ridiculous? I

weakened this morning and bought you a mobile phone after all.'

'Oh Marion!'

'But I'm not sure I'll give it to you now – though at least it would mean I could phone you to check where you are. You've driven me demented today, April.'

'I'm sorry. I didn't plan it to be this way. I just kept thinking about the past, and my mother putting me in the dustbin and – oh Marion, you'll never guess!'

She draws in her breath sharply. 'Your mother? You haven't *found* her?'

'No. No, I've found Frankie, you know, the one who found me in the dustbin.'

I explain that he's coming to meet me at The Pizza Place. Marion fusses and takes down his phone number and insists that she's going to come too.

'But it will take you ages, and you sound ever so tired.'

'I am!'

'I'm sorry, Marion.'

'And I shall probably make you even sorrier by the time I'm through with you!'

'I bet you wish you'd never taken me on.' I stop suddenly. 'Is that why you talked to Elaine? Do you want to get rid of me?'

'Oh April! Of course I don't! You're mine.'

'You're mine too,' I say.

Marion is crying too when we say goodbye.

I mop my eyes, wipe my nose, and walk out towards The Pizza Place. I think about my mother stumbling along fourteen years ago, about to give birth to me. It's starting to seem so shadowy and unreal.

I don't know if she really is the way I imagine. She could be any woman anywhere. I could sit next to her on a bus or brush past her in a shop and neither of us would know. Maybe it's silly to think a birth mother so important when the birth is the only thing that connects you.

It's weird the way I've loved her all these years. Maybe I should have hated her for dumping me in that dustbin. I know I'd never do that to any baby of mine, no matter what. I'll keep her and love her and hold her tight. I'll be a proper mum to *my* baby.

I haven't got a mum. But one day I can be my *child*'s mum.

A real mum.

I go into The Pizza Place. The waiter smiles at me, shows me to a table, and asks me if I'm on my own.

I hesitate.

'I've got . . . family coming later,' I say.

QUICK QUIZ!

You've finished reading *Dustbin Baby*, but how much of the story do you remember?

1. Which friend's hairstyle does April copy?

2. What sort of flowers does Marion give April as part of her birthday breakfast?

3. April hopes she'll get a mobile phone for her birthday, but Marion gives her a pair of earrings instead. What special stone are they?

4. April was born in the alleyway behind a restaurant – what is it called?

5. Which hospital does Frankie take baby April to?

6. April's pretty friend Hannah goes on a date with a really popular boy – what's his name?

7. April meets a character from another of Jacqueline Wilson's books in *Dustbin Baby*! Who is it and which book is she from?

8. When April was adopted by Janet and Daniel, what new first name did they choose for her?

9. When April first meets Marion – or Miss Bean, as she knows her back then – they argue over a piece of work Miss Bean sets the class. What is it?

10. Frankie leaves a special message for April in the alleyway, in the hope that she'll get in touch with him. What is it?

ANSWERS

1. Hannah 2. Irises 3. Moonstones 4. The Pizza Place 5. St Mary's Hospital 6. Grant Lacey 7. Tanya from BAD GIRLS 8. Danielle 9. A family tree 10. PLEASE CALL, BABY

THINGS TO THINK ABOUT

1. *Dustbin Baby* begins and ends in the same way – with April in the restaurant, waiting for Frankie to arrive. To start with, of course, we don't know who she is waiting for – who did you imagine this might be? Did you think this might have been April's real mother? Were you surprised, pleased, or even disappointed when you realized it wasn't?

2. April often has very mixed feelings towards Marion, the teacher who became her foster mother. What do you think of Marion as a character, and as a parent? Is April lucky to have found Marion, or do you think she's too old-fashioned and out of touch to bring up a fourteen-year-old girl?

3. April's life began with a very unusual and extreme decision by her birth mother – the decision to abandon her baby. What do you think of this action? Are there any circumstances under which you think this could have been the right thing to do?

4. April has imagined, in detail, the scenario that might have happened when her mother gave birth to her. Discuss the other options, and create your own version of what might have happened. Was April's mother very young? Did she have a boyfriend or a husband, or was she alone? Do you think her own parents knew she was about to be a mother – or perhaps she had no parents?

5. Imagine that April's birth mother chose to keep her baby, rather than abandoning her. How would April's life and character have been affected by this?

6. Many people who are adopted decide to search for their biological parents later in life, even if they have grown up with kind and loving adoptive families. Why do you think they feel so compelled to find the people they are related to by blood?

7. April comments that Frankie isn't allowed to keep her, even though her own mother would have been allowed to have her back, because 'blood is thicker than water'. What do you think of this statement? Do you think April believes this herself?

8. Hannah and Cathy, April's friends at school, often comment on the fact that April copies them in a lot of ways. Why do you think April might struggle to see herself as an individual?

9. Marion wants April to go to university and study History. What it is about this particular subject that you think Marion sees as being right for April? What do you think the future holds in store for her?

10. When April arranges to meet Frankie and Marion at The Pizza Place, she tells the waiter she's 'got family coming later'. What do you think of her notion of 'family' here?

APRIL'S BIRTHDAY MEMORIES

April has a memory of being a tiny baby,
and being discovered by Frankie in the dustbin.
Do you think she could really remember back this
far, or was she just imagining what she thought
may have happened? What do you think the day
of your own birth was like? Describe it here.

_____

_____

_____

_____

_____

_____

_____

_____

_____

_____

_____

_____

_____

_____

_____

APRIL FOOLS!

April was named after the month of her birth, but hates the fact that she was born on 1st April – known as April Fools' Day. What's the best prank you've ever played on this day?

_____

_____

_____

The earliest record of 1st April being linked to 'foolishness' appears in *The Canterbury Tales* by Geoffrey Chaucer, published over six hundred years ago in 1392.

In France and Italy, children and adults traditionally tack paper fish on each other's back as a trick and shout 'April fish!' – that's *'Poisson d'avril!' in* French and and *'Pesce d'aprile!'* in Italian.

What's the most famous April Fools' Day prank ever? Some people argue it's the 'spaghetti tree hoax'. In 1957, the TV presenter Richard Dimbleby fronted a documentary on *Panorama*, in which he told the audience about the 'spaghetti harvest' and showed them the spaghetti 'growing' and being 'dried' in the sun. Millions of people fell for it – and even rang the BBC asking how they could grow their own spaghetti trees!

YOUR FAMILY TREE

Most people can fill in their family trees for one or two generations back. How much do you know about your own family? Talk to your parents, grandparents, aunts, uncles and even family friends to find out more, and draw your family tree here.

If you have enjoyed reading
DUSTBIN BABY, you might also like
MY SISTER JODIE.

Read on for the first two chapters . . .

'I told you so!' said Mum triumphantly.

1

Jodie. It was the first word I ever said. Most babies lisp *Mumma* or *Dadda* or *Drinkie* or *Teddy*. Maybe everyone names the thing they love best. I said *Jodie*, my sister. OK, I said *Dodie* because I couldn't say my Js properly, but I knew what I meant.

I said her name first every morning.

'Jodie? Jodie! Wake up. *Please* wake up!'

She was hopeless in the mornings. I always woke up early – six o'clock, sometimes even earlier. When I was little, I'd delve around my bed to find my three night-time teddies, and then take them for a dawn trek up and down my duvet. I put my knees up and they'd clamber up the mountain and then slide down. Then they'd burrow back to base camp and tuck into their pretend porridge for breakfast.

I wasn't allowed to eat anything so early. I wasn't even allowed to get up. I was fine once I could read. Sometimes I got through a whole book before the alarm went off. Then I'd lie staring at the ceiling, making up my own stories. I'd wait as long as I could, and then I'd climb into Jodie's bed and whisper her name, give her a little shake and start telling her the new story. They were always about two sisters. They went through an old wardrobe into a magic land, or they went to stage school and became famous actresses, or they went to a ball in beautiful long dresses and danced in glass slippers.

It was always hard to get Jodie to wake up properly. It was as if she'd fallen down a long dark tunnel in the night. It took her ages to crawl back to the surface. But eventually she'd open one eye and her arm went round me automatically. I'd cuddle up and carry on telling her the story. I had to keep nudging her and saying, 'You *are* still awake, aren't you, Jodie?'

'I'm wide awake,' she mumbled, but I had to give her little prods to make sure.

When she *was* awake, she'd sometimes take over the story. She'd tell me how the two sisters ruled over the magic land as twin queens, and they acted in their own daily television soap, and they danced with each other all evening at the ball until way past midnight.

Jodie's stories were always much better than mine. I begged her to write them down but she couldn't be bothered.

'*You* write them down for me,' she said. 'You're the one that wants to be the writer.'

I wanted to write my own stories and illustrate them too.

'I can help you with the ideas,' said Jodie. 'You can do all the drawings and I'll do the colouring in.'

'So long as you do it carefully in the right

2

colours,' I said, because Jodie nearly always went over the lines, and sometimes she coloured faces green and hair blue just for the fun of it.

'OK, Miss Picky,' said Jodie. 'I'll help you out but that won't be my *real* job. I'm going to be an actress. That's what I really want to do. Imagine, standing there, all lit up, with everyone listening, hanging on your every word!'

'Maybe one of my stories could be turned into a play and then you could have the star part.'

'Yeah, I'll be an overnight success and be offered mega millions to make movies and we'll live together in a huge great mansion,' said Jodie.

'What does a mansion look like?' I said. 'Can it have towers? Can our room be right at the top of a tower?'

'*All* the rooms are our rooms, but we'll share a very special room right at the top of a tower, only I'm not going to let you grow your hair any longer.' She pulled one of my plaits. 'I don't want you tossing it out of the window and letting any wicked old witches climb up it.' Jodie nudged me. She had started to have a lot of arguments with our mother. She often called her a witch – or worse – but only under her breath.

'Don't worry, I'll keep my plaits safely tied up. No access for wicked witches,' I said, giggling, though I felt a bit mean to Mum.

'What about handsome princes?'

'*Definitely* not,' I said. 'It'll be just you and me in Mansion Towers, living happily ever after.'

It was just our silly early-morning game, though I took it more seriously than Jodie. I drew our imaginary mansion, often slicing it open like a

3

doll's house so I could illustrate every room. I gave us a huge black velvet sofa with two big black toy pumas lolling at either end. We had two real black cats for luck lapping from little bowls in the kitchen, two poodles curled up together in their dog basket, while twin black ponies grazed in a paddock beside our rose garden. I coloured each rose carefully and separately, deep red, salmon, peach, very pale pink, apricot and yellow. I even tried to do every blade of grass individually but had to see sense after dabbing delicately for half an hour, my hand aching.

I gave us a four-poster bed with red velvet curtains and a ruby chandelier, and one wall was a vast television screen. We had a turquoise swimming pool in the basement (with our twin pet dolphins) and a roof garden between the towers where skylarks and bluebirds skimmed the blossom trees.

I printed the title of each of our books in the library in weeny writing and drew every item of food on our kitchen shelves. I gave us a playroom with a trampoline and a trapeze and a jukebox, and one of those machines you get at the seaside where you have to manoeuvre a crane to pick up little furry teddies. I drew tiny teddies every colour of the rainbow, and I had a shelf of big teddies in our bedroom, and a shelf of old-fashioned dolls with real hair and glass eyes, and a splendid rocking horse big enough for both of us to ride on.

I talked about it to Jodie as if we'd really live there one day. Sometimes I imagined it so vividly it seemed like a real place. I just had to work out which road to take out of town and then I'd round a corner and spot the towers. I'd run fast, through the elaborate wrought-iron gates, up to the front door with the big lion's-head knocker. I'd know how to press the lion's snout with my finger and the door would spring open and I'd step inside and Jodie would be there waiting for me.

I wasn't stupid, I knew it wasn't really real, but it felt as if it might be all the same.

Then one morning at breakfast everything changed. I was sitting at the kitchen table nibbling at a honey sandwich. I liked opening the sandwich up and licking the honey, letting it ooze over my tongue, but I did it quickly and furtively when Mum wasn't looking. She was very strict about table manners. She was forever nagging Jodie about sitting up straight and spooning her corn-flakes up quietly without clanking the spoon against the bowl. Jodie slumped further into an S shape and clanked until she nearly cracked the china. Mum took hold of her by the shoulders and gave her a good shaking.

'Stop winding me up, you contrary little whatsit,' she said, going *shake shake shake*.

Jodie's head rocked backwards and forwards on her stiff shoulders.

'You're hurting her!' said Dad, putting down his *Daily Express* and looking anxious.

'She's not hurting me,' Jodie gasped, waggling her head herself, and then she started da-da-da-ing part of that weird old 'Bohemian Rhapsody' song when everyone bangs their heads to the music.

'Stop that silly row! I suppose you think you're funny,' said Mum.

But Dad was laughing and shaking his own

5

head. 'You're a right head-case, our Jodie,' he said.

'Trust you to encourage her, Joe,' said Mum. 'Why do you always have to take Jodie's side?'

'Because I'm my daddy's girl,' said Jodie, batting her eyelashes at Dad.

She was too. She was always in trouble now, bunking off school and staying out late. Mum could shake her head until it snapped right off her shoulders but she couldn't control her. But Dad could still sometimes make her hang her head and cry because she'd worried them so.

He'd never say a bad word against Jodie.

'It's not her fault. OK, she's always been a bit headstrong, but she's basically been a good little kid. She's just got in with the wrong crowd now, that's all. She's no worse than any of her mates at school,' he said.

'Quite!' said Mum. 'Moorcroft's a rubbish school. The kids aren't taught properly at all. They just run wild. Half of them are in trouble with the police. It was the biggest mistake in the world letting our Jodie go there. She's heading for trouble in a big way. Just *look* at her!'

I thought Jodie looked wonderful. She used to have pale mousy hair in meek little plaits but now she'd dyed her hair a dark orangy-red with streaky gold bits. She wore it in a funny spiky ponytail with a fringe she'd cut herself. Dad said she looked like a pot of marmalade – he'd spread her on toast if she didn't watch out. Mum said Jodie had ruined her hair and now she looked tough and tarty. Jodie was thrilled. She *wanted* to look tough and tarty.

Then there were her ears. Jodie had been begging Mum to let her have her ears pierced. Mum always said no, so last year Jodie went off and got her ears pierced herself. She kept going back, so there are five extra little rings up one ear.

'You've got more perforations than a blooming colander,' said Dad.

Mum was outraged at each and every new piercing.

'Hey, hey, they're only pretty little earrings,' said Dad. 'It's not as if she's got a nose-stud or a tattoo.'

'*Yet!*' Jodie whispered to me.

She'd tried going to a tattoo parlour but they said she was too young. She inked butterflies and blue-birds and daisy chains up and down her arms and legs with my felt pens instead. She looked incredible in her underwear with her red-gold hair and her earrings and her fake tattoos – but her clothes were mostly as dull and little-girly as mine. Jodie didn't have enough money to buy much herself. Mum was in charge when it came to clothes-buying. Dad didn't dare slip Jodie some money any more. She'd told him this story about her clunky school shoes rubbing her toes sore, so he gave her forty pounds for some new ones. She bought her first pair of proper high heels, fantastic flashy sparkly red shoes, and clacked happily round the house in them, deaf to Mum's fury. She let me try them out. They were so high I immediately fell over, twisting my ankle, but I didn't care. I felt like Dorothy wearing her ruby slippers in *The Wizard of Oz*.

Jodie was wearing the clunky school shoes this morning, and the grey Moorcroft uniform. She'd done her best to customize it, hitching up the skirt as high as she could, and she'd pinned funny

7

badges on her blazer. She'd inked little cartoon characters all over her school tie. Mum started on a new nag about the tie, but she interrupted herself when she heard the letterbox bang.

'Post, Pearl. Go and get it, pet.'

I'm Pearl. When I was born, Mum called me her precious little pearl and the name stuck. I was born prematurely and had to stay tucked up in an incubator for more than a month. I only weighed a kilo and was still so little when they were allowed to bring me home that Dad could cradle me in one of his hands. They were very worried about Jodie's reaction to me. She was a harem-scarem little girl who always twisted off her dolls' heads and kicked her teddies – but she was incredibly careful with me. She held me very gently and kissed my little wrinkled forehead and stroked my fluffy hair and said I was the best little sister in the whole world.

I picked up the post. A catalogue for Mum (she wrote off for them all – clothes, furniture, commemorative plates, reproduction china dolls – anything she thought would add a touch of class to our household) and a letter addressed to Mr and Mrs Wells – Mum and Dad. A proper letter in a big white envelope, not a bill.

I wondered who would be writing to them. I hoped it wasn't a letter from the head of Moorcroft complaining about Jodie. I knew she and her friends had been caught smoking once or twice, and sometimes they sneaked out of school at lunch time to go and get chips and didn't always bother to go back again. Jodie didn't *like* smoking, she told me privately; it made her feel sick and dizzy, and she also said the school chips were much better than the pale greasy ones in polystyrene pouches from the chippy, but she was trying to keep in with Marie and Siobhan and Shanice. They were the three toughest girls in Jodie's class. If you kept them on your side, you were laughing.

'Pearl?' Mum called.

I fingered the letter in my hand, wondering if I should stick it up under my school sweater until we could steam it open in private. But then Mum came out into the hall and saw the letter before I could whip it out of sight. She barely glanced at the catalogue, even though it was the one for little enamel pill boxes, one of her favourites. She took hold of the letter and ran her finger under the seal.

'It's for Dad too,' I said quickly. He'd be softer on Jodie; he always was.

'Mr *and* Mrs,' said Mum, opening it.

There was a letter inside and some sort of brochure. I peered at it as best I could. I saw the words *boarding school*. My heart started beating fast. *Boarding school, boarding school, boarding school!* Oh God, they were going to send Jodie to boarding school. I wouldn't be able to bear it.

'No, Mum!' I said, my voice a little squeak.

Mum was reading the letter intently, her head moving from side to side. 'No what?' she murmured, still reading.

'Don't send Jodie away!' I said.

Mum blinked at me. 'Don't be silly,' she said, walking back into the living room. She flapped the letter in front of Dad's face.

'Look, Joe, look!' she said. 'Here it is in black and white!'

9

'Well I'll be damned!' said Dad.

'I told you so!' said Mum triumphantly.

Jodie pushed her cornflakes bowl away and got up from the table, taking no notice.

'Sit down, Jodie,' said Mum.

'But I'll be late for school,' said Jodie.

'It won't matter just this once,' said Mum. 'Sit *down*! You too, Pearl. Your dad and I have got something to tell you.'

'What?' said Jodie, sitting back on the very edge of her chair. 'You're getting a divorce?'

'Don't be ridiculous!'

'You're going to have another baby?'

'Stop it now! Just button that lip of yours for two seconds.'

Jodie mimed buttoning her lips. I copied her, zipping mine.

Mum glared. 'Now, don't start copying your sister, miss! Shame on you, Jodie, you're a bad example. It's just as well you'll be making a move. I can't believe how badly you behave nowadays.'

'You *are* sending her off to this boarding school!' I wailed.

'*What* boarding school?' said Jodie, looking startled. 'You mean you're getting rid of me?'

'No, no, of course we're not,' said Dad. 'We're *all* going. I've got a new job. We both have, your mum and me.'

We stared at them. New jobs? At a *school*? Dad worked as a carpenter for a small building firm and Mum was a waitress at Jenny's Teashop opposite the town hall.

'Are you going to be teachers?' I said doubtfully.

Dad burst out laughing. 'Heaven help any pupils

if I had to teach them their reading and writing! No, no, sweetheart, I'm going to be the school caretaker and your mum's going to be the school cook. We saw this advert for a married couple and it seemed like we might fit the bill.'

'It's time for a move,' said Mum. 'We need to get you girls away to a decent environment where you can grow up into little ladies.'

Jodie made a very unladylike noise. 'We like it here, don't we, Pearl? We don't want to go to some awful jolly-hockey-sticks boarding school.'

I picked up the school brochure. I shivered when I saw the coloured photograph of the huge grey Victorian building. My fingers traced the gables and turrets and the tower. It was called Melchester College, but it was just like my dream-world Mansion Towers.

'Look!' I said, pointing. 'Look, Jodie!'

Jodie looked too. She bit her lip, fiddling with the little row of earrings running down her left ear. 'We'd live *there*?' she said.

'There's a special caretaker's flat,' said Dad.

'It's got all the mod cons even though it all looks so old fashioned,' said Mum.

'So you've both been to see it? When?' said Jodie. 'Why didn't you tell us? Did you fix it all up behind our backs?'

'Hey, hey, none of it's been fixed up,' said Dad. 'We haven't even been to see the college ourselves. We went to this interview at a hotel in London while you two were at school. We didn't say anything because we didn't want to get your hopes up. To tell the truth I never thought in a million years they'd take me on. I mean, I'm fine with wood but I'm a bit of a botcher when it comes to plumbing or painting.'

'Don't be silly, Joe, you're a skilled carpenter and a fine odd-job man. What else could they possibly want?' said Mum.

'No, no, I think we got the job because of your cooking and management skills,' said Dad, reaching out and patting her hand. 'You were dead impressive at the interview, Sharon – the way you had that list of sample meals all sorted out, that was fantastic.'

'Where *is* this Melchester College? Why can't I still go to Moorcroft? I don't mind a long bus ride,' said Jodie.

'It would have to be a *very* long bus ride – it's a good hundred miles away, right out in the country,' said Mum. 'No, you'll be moving, thank heaven.'

'No I'm not,' said Jodie. 'I'm staying with all my mates at Moorcroft.'

'I hate that word. It's *friends*,' said Mum. 'And that's the whole point of us moving away. I'm sick to death of you hanging around with that deadbeat crowd, acquiring bad habits. We're moving in the nick of time, before you start seriously studying for your GCSEs and before Pearl starts secondary school. You girls need to make something of yourselves – and now we're giving you a golden opportunity.' Mum stroked the shiny brochure. 'Melchester College,' she said slowly and reverently, as if it was a magic word like *Abracadabra*.

'Melchester College!' Jodie mocked. She glanced at the brochure. 'It looks dead posh. It says it's for four- to thirteen-year-olds. Who could send a little kid of *four* to boarding school?'

'It's a day school too; not everyone boards. It's very select, naturally. It prides itself on the teacher/pupil ratio and the outstanding pastoral care,' said Mum, quoting.

'So what does that mean?' said Jodie.

'It means it's a very good school,' Mum snapped. 'It costs a great deal of money to send a child there. It's a wonderful opportunity for you two.'

'You mean we're supposed to have lessons there?' said Jodie.

'That's the whole point!' said Mum. 'You've learned nothing this last year at Moorcroft. We're going to have you repeating Year Eight, getting properly taught.'

'I'm not repeating a year with a lot of posh kids all *younger* than me!' said Jodie.

'But given the right coaching, you could pass this Common Entrance exam and win a scholarship to one of the public schools,' said Mum.

'*What?* Are you crazy, Mum? I'm not going. Ab-so-lute-ly no way!' Jodie was shouting.

'Hey, hey, Jodie, listen to me,' said Dad. 'We'll be there all through the summer holidays so you'll have lots of time to settle in. I know you're going to love it when you get there.'

'I won't, I'll hate it. I'm not going. You can't make me.'

'Of course we can. You'll do as we say. You're our daughter.'

'I wish I wasn't! Maybe I'm not. Maybe you adopted me and that's why I'm so different and never feel like I fit in,' Jodie yelled.

'Don't start, Jodie, you're doing my head in,' said Dad. 'Don't spoil it all. Like your mum says, it's a wonderful opportunity. We thought you girls would be thrilled to bits.'

'Well, we're not, are we, Pearl?' said Jodie. She looked at me.

I looked back at her helplessly.

'Do you really want to go there?' she asked, astonished.

I struggled. I nearly always copied Jodie, even if it got me into trouble. But we didn't always have the same ideas, although we were such close sisters. Jodie had hated it at Moorcroft at first. She'd been horribly teased about her girly plaits and neat uniform and nice manners. She had cut off her hair and changed her clothes and learned to talk tough so now she was fine, one of the gang. Some of the kids were even scared of her. I'd be scared of her myself if she wasn't my sister.

I knew *I* wouldn't be able to manage Moorcroft. I had nightmares about going there in September. I got horribly teased *now*, in Year Six in the Juniors. I was still very small for my age and looked very babyish; I worked hard and came top in class; I was useless at sport; I always had my head in a book; I blushed whenever a teacher talked to me in class; I never knew what to *say* to all the others. It was as if I had an arrow up above me: *Tease this kid!*

Melchester College looked like the sort of place where *everyone* wore proper uniform and worked hard and tried to come top. And even if the lessons were awful, Jodie and I would still be living in a real-life version of Mansion Towers. Maybe we'd even be able to share a tower room!

'You *can't* want to go there, Pearl,' said Jodie.

'I think I do,' I mumbled.

14

'Well, I *don't*,' said Jodie. She folded her arms. 'You go, Pearl. Fine. But no one's going to make *me* go there.'

'I can't go without you!' I said, starting to cry.

'There now, you've reduced your sister to tears. I hope you're proud of yourself,' said Mum. 'Why do you always have to spoil things for everyone? Poor little Pearl. Say sorry to her, Jodie, she's sobbing her heart out.'

'I think you should all say sorry to *me*, trying to force me off to this stupid snobby school. I'm not going. I'm not changing my mind, not in a million years,' Jodie shouted, and she slammed out of the door.

But that night when I started crying again in bed, she sighed and slid under the duvet beside me.

'Stop all that blubbing, silly. Do you really really really want to go to Melchester College, Pearl?'

'Yes. But not without you,' I sobbed.

'You're going to have to stand on your own two feet *some* time,' said Jodie. 'But all right – I'll come too. Just so as I can look after you. OK?'

'You'll really come to Melchester College?' I said, putting my arms round her neck and hugging her tight.

'Yes. I'll hate it. But I'll come, just for you,' said Jodie. 'Now quit strangling me and snuggle up and go to sleep.'

'Drunk!' Mum exploded, and she slapped Jodie's face.

2

I wonder how many times we said the words
Melchester College over the next few weeks. Mum
tried out special traditional school-dinner recipes
every day: shepherd's pie, toad-in-the-hole, meat
loaf. They were all pretty horrible but she did real
puddings too, jam roly-poly and treacle pudding
and sherry trifle, and they were absolutely
wonderful. Dad kissed his fingertips and said each
dish was truly scrumptious. He even sang the
'Truly Scrumptious' song from *Chitty Chitty Bang
Bang* to Mum, and she giggled and did a little
dance, swishing her skirts and twirling around.
They were fooling about like teenagers all of a
sudden, not acting like Mum and Dad at all.

Mum didn't nag Jodie so much, although she
got really really mad when Jodie went out with
Marie, Siobhan and Shanice on Thursday night,
supposedly to a church youth club. Jodie promised
she'd be in around half ten. She didn't get home

until way past midnight, wobbling in her high red heels.

'Drunk!' Mum exploded, and she slapped Jodie's face.

I was sitting at the top of the stairs, shivering in my nightie, anxiously gnawing at a hangnail on my thumb. The slap was such a shock I ripped the hangnail halfway down my thumb, making it bleed. It was so sore that tears sprang to my eyes. Jodie didn't cry, though when she came up to our bedroom, one side of her face was still bright scarlet from the slap.

'Oh, Jodie! Are you *really* drunk?' I asked, wondering whether she was going to start reeling round and falling over like comic drunks on the telly.

'Not really *really* drunk,' said Jodie, peering at herself in the mirror. 'I did feel a bit weird when we came out of the club, but then I puked into the gutter and I felt better.'

'Did they have real drinks at Shanice's youth club then?' I said.

'As if!' said Jodie. 'We weren't *at* her youth club. We went proper clubbing – the under-eighteens night at the Rendezvous.'

'You never!'

'You *didn't*, dear – you've got to remember to speak nicely now you're going to Melchester College,' said Jodie, imitating Mum's voice.

'Ssh, Mum will hear!' I said, giggling. 'So what was it *like*, clubbing? Was it scary? Did you dance with any boys?'

'I danced with heaps of boys,' said Jodie. 'More than Shanice and them, and they got a bit narked and went off without me. Marie said I was a slag because I let this boy snog my face off.'

'You *never*! Didn't. Whatever. *Which* boy?'

'I don't know. He told me his name but I couldn't hear it properly because it was so noisy. Marty or Barty. Maybe it was Farty?'

'Jodie!'

'He wouldn't leave me alone and I let him slobber all over me just to annoy Marie because she'd said she fancied him. She was welcome to him actually. To all of them. Just as well I couldn't hear them talk. It was just rubbish anyway. I don't like the way boys just want to dance and snog and touch you up. They don't want to be *mates*.'

'I don't like boys either,' I said. 'Some of the girls in my class have got boyfriends. They say I'm a baby.'

'Well, I'm a baby too, because *I* haven't got a boyfriend, and I don't want one either,' said Jodie, rubbing her lips fiercely with the back of her hand.

She flopped down on her bed and pulled the duvet up to her chin even though she was fully dressed, with her high heels still on.

'Night-night, Pearly Girly,' she said, closing her eyes.

'Hey, you've still got your shoes on!'

I knelt on her bed and wiggled her shoes off her feet. She had a hole in her tights, her big toe sticking through comically. I waggled it and Jodie giggled sleepily.

'Give over. Come to bed, Pearl,' she said, reaching out and pulling me in beside her. 'You're freezing, like a little snowman!' she said, cuddling me close.

'We don't ever have to have boyfriends, do we,

Jodie? We can still have our own place together, can't we?'

'Mansion Towers,' Jodie mumbled.

'I can't believe we're going to live in Melchester College,' I said.

I closed my eyes, nestling against Jodie in her warm bed. I saw us wandering the grounds of the college together, having picnics on the lawn, paddling in the lake, picking raspberries and strawberries in the kitchen garden . . .

We didn't have any kind of garden at home, because Dad's workshop took up all of our back yard. He pottered out there most evenings, but I don't think he ever did much *work*. He watched his little portable telly, brewed himself a cup of tea and enjoyed a bit of peace and quiet. Mum was forever on to him to make her new kitchen units but he never seemed to get round to it, just managing the odd cupboard or shelf.

I'd begged him to make me a doll's house. I'd hoped for a miniature Mansion Towers, but he made me a small square four-roomed house with a wobbly chimney stuck on top. He'd tried so hard, sticking special red-checked paper on the outside to look like bricks. I gave him a big hug and kiss, but privately I thought the house was hideous. I furnished it with a plastic bed and chair and tables and tried to play games with a family of pink plastic people, but it wouldn't become real. I had much more fun playing house in a cardboard shoebox with a paper family.

Jodie had never wanted a doll's house. When she was little, she'd asked Dad to make her a rocket, which was a challenge for him. He struggled hard, because he could never say no to Jodie. He handed over his rocket proudly. It was hollow, with a little hinged door, pointy at one end, touched up with shiny grey paint. It looked like a big wooden fish. Jodie held it in her hand, looking puzzled.

'What *is* it, Dad?'

'It's your rocket, sweetheart,' said Dad.

Jodie wasn't good at hiding her feelings. Her face crumpled up. 'But it's much too small. I can't get in it!' she wailed. 'I want to go up to the moon!'

'Daddy can't make you a real rocket, you noodle!' said Mum.

Jodie howled. Mum laughed at her. Even Dad found it funny, I wasn't there – I wasn't even born yet – but the story had become family history, passed down like a folk tale.

We found the rocket at the bottom of Jodie's wardrobe when we were sorting through all our things for the big move.

'My rocket!' said Jodie, dusting it with an old sock. She made it swoop in and out of her clothes, and then she stood back and chucked it into the air so that its pointy wooden nose hit the ceiling with a satisfying *thuck*. It made a little dent in the ceiling plaster and then hurtled back to earth. Jodie caught it one-handed.

'We have lift-off, brief landing on ceiling and perfect re-entry,' she said.

'What was that noise?' said Mum, bursting into the room, a pile of our old clothes in her arms.

'Nothing, Mum,' we chorused.

'Well come on, girls, get a move on. Get all those old toys sorted into cardboard boxes, then Dad will take them to the hospice shop in the car.'

Mum glanced up at the ceiling. 'Where did that mark come from?' she said, frowning.

'What mark?' we said in unison.

'You two!' said Mum, but she was in too cheery a mood to get really angry. We heard her humming 'Truly Scrumptious' as she went back into her own room.

'I don't know what to keep and what to chuck,' I said, stirring all my toys. 'I never play with my Barbies now, or my cut-out paper dolls, or my giant set of wax crayons – they're just for babies, but I don't really want to throw them *out*.'

It was easier for Jodie. Most of her old toys were broken. Her old Barbies had skinhead haircuts and tattoos and assorted amputations; her teddy had led such an adventurous life that his head was hanging off his shoulders by a thread. Her crayons were stumps and her paints a sludgy mess.

'Junk, junk, junketty junk,' she chanted as she threw them rhythmically into a black plastic rubbish bag.

She grew wilder, throwing in her cream clutch bag and cream pumps, her pink crocheted poncho, her white fluffy towelling dressing gown, her floral toothmug and flannel and washbag, her pink alarm clock in the shape of a heart.

'Jodie! You'll hurt Mum's feelings,' I said.

'She never minds hurting mine,' said Jodie.

'They were presents from her.'

'Yeah, but they're all stuff *she* likes, not me.'

'I quite like them too,' I said. 'Can I have your dressing gown if you don't want it?'

'Sure,' said Jodie, wrapping it round me. She

22

laughed. 'You look like a polar bear. Here, bear, want a fishy?'

She pretended to feed me the wooden rocket, and then chucked it carelessly into the black plastic bag – but that night I heard her scrabbling in the bag, searching for something. I kept quiet. The next morning I saw she'd wedged the rocket beside her red shoes in her small suitcase of treasured possessions.

We lived with cases and cardboard boxes all around us for days, never quite sure where anything was, suddenly needing something that was packed right away. Dad was out all day and half the night, trying to complete all the bookshelves and bathroom cabinets on his order book. He had a farewell do with his mates at work and came home all tearful, saying they were a cracking bunch of lads, like brothers to him.

We had a farewell Sunday lunch with Dad's real brother, Uncle Jack, and Aunty Pauline and our two little cousins, Ashleigh and Aimee, and Dad's mum came too. They all wished us the best, and Gran kept saying how much she'd miss us, though whenever we went round to her house she was always telling us off, especially Jodie.

Mum didn't say goodbye to any of her family. She didn't keep in touch. She always sniffed when she spoke about them. Jodie and I would have loved to meet this other gran who always 'went down the boozer', and the granddad who'd been on benefit all his life, and we especially wanted to meet the uncle who'd been 'in and out of the nick', but Mum had left home at seventeen and never gone back. She did her last shift at Jenny's Teashop, coming home with a carved wooden spoon and a new apron with

SUPERCOOK embroidered in white across the chest –
gifts from her regular customers.

Jodie missed school altogether for the last couple
of weeks. Marie and Siobhan and Shanice had
turned against her and it was simpler and safer to
keep out of their way. Jodie said she mooched
around the town in the mornings, ate the packed
lunch Mum made for her down by the river, and
then mostly hung around the park until it was time
to come home. She liked the children's playground.
She always loved little kids. She'd had plenty of
practice looking after me. They all ran at her as
soon as they spotted her, hanging on her arms,
begging her to pick them up, to whirl them about,
to give them a push on the swings or help them up
and down the little slide. The mums made a fuss of
her too because they could sit on the bench and
chat amongst themselves while Jodie leaped about
like Mary Poppins on skates.

'Maybe I'll be a nursery nurse when I'm older,'
Jodie said happily. 'I seem to have the knack for it.
Or I could be a nanny. Or maybe I'll just have heaps
of kids of my own.'

'I thought you said you didn't want to get
married,' I said.

'I don't! You don't have to have a husband to have
lots of children,' said Jodie, winking at me.

'Mum would go spare if she heard you saying
that,' I said.

'Mum goes spare at *everything* I say,' said Jodie.

'What if she finds out you're bunking off from
school?'

'She won't. I'm leaving anyway, so what does it
matter?' Jodie said carelessly.

24

She didn't bother to go back to say goodbye to anyone. I didn't actually say goodbye to many people at my school either. I didn't really have any proper friends. I did say a proper goodbye to my teacher, Mrs Lambert, because she was always kind to me.

'I'm so happy for you that you're going to this boarding school, Pearl. It's a wonderful opportunity. You're a very bright girl. I know you'll make the most of it.' She straightened up, shaking her head now. 'What about that big sister of yours? How does she feel about going?'

I shrugged awkwardly.

'I was very fond of Jodie, though she was always a handful,' she said, smiling. 'Still, maybe she'll turn into a lovely young lady at boarding school.'

The incredible stories of Hetty Feather, the Victorian foundling determined to find her real family and start a better life!

There are oodles of incredible Jacqueline Wilson books to enjoy! Tick off the ones you have read, so you know which ones to look for next!

- ☐ The Dinosaur's Packed Lunch
- ☐ The Monster Story-Teller

- ☐ The Cat Mummy
- ☐ Lizzie Zipmouth
- ☐ Sleepovers

- ☑ Bad Girls
- ☐ The Bed and Breakfast Star
- ☑ Best Friends
- ☐ Big Day Out
- ☐ Buried Alive!
- ☐ Candyfloss
- ☐ Clean Break
- ☐ Cliffhanger
- ☐ Cookie
- ☐ The Dare Game
- ☐ The Diamond Girls
- ☐ Double Act
- ☐ Emerald Star
- ☐ Glubbslyme
- ☐ Hetty Feather
- ☐ The Illustrated Mum
- ☐ Jacky Daydream
- ☐ Lily Alone

- ☐ Little Darlings
- ☐ Lola Rose
- ☐ The Longest Whale Song
- ☐ The Lottie Project
- ☐ Midnight
- ☑ The Mum-Minder
- ☐ Queenie
- ☐ Sapphire Battersea
- ☑ Secrets
- ☐ Starring Tracy Beaker
- ☐ The Story of Tracy Beaker
- ☐ The Suitcase Kid
- ☑ Vicky Angel
- ☐ The Worry Website
- ☑ The Worst Thing About My Sister

FOR OLDER READERS:

- ☑ Dustbin Baby
- ☐ Girls In Love
- ☐ Girls In Tears
- ☐ Girls Out Late
- ☐ Girls Under Pressure
- ☐ Kiss
- ☐ Love Lessons
- ☐ My Secret Diary
- ☐ My Sister Jodie